Diana Marie DuBois

AN
UNEXPECTED
HERO

A LEGACY FALLS NOVELLA

Thank you for taking the time to read my novella from the Legacy Falls Project.

All reviews are appreciated.

If you would like to find out more about the Legacy Falls Project, please join our Facebook page:
https://www.facebook.com/groups/1095597557149707/
The Legacy Fall Project Includes:

Platform Four by Eden Butler
Behind My Charade by Skye Turner
Her Southern Temptation by Trish Leger
Dear Dixie by JL Baldwin
Iron Heart by Madison Street
Beyond the Ghosts bye Jody Pardo
An Unexpected Hero by Diana Marie DuBois
Home by Morgan Jane

Diana Marie DuBois

AN UNEXPECTED HERO

A LEGACY FALLS NOVELLA

Published by Three Danes Publishing L.L.C.

Cover art by Anya Kelleye
http://www.anyakelleye.com/
Cover photo CJC Photography
Model BT Urruela
Edited by Maxine Horton Bringenberg
Beth Lake

Note to Readers

I hope you enjoy my story *An Unexpected Hero*. When a soldier comes home, we never truly know what goes on in their heads when they return. Every day is an ongoing battle. Thankfully for my character, he had a family that had his back continually and tried to help him. What we must remember is that they fight for our freedom every day. From day one of this project I wanted BT Urruela on the cover. The more I listened to his story, the more I knew I had made the right decision in having him portray my character. Like my character in the book he rose above the constraints of what life was now like for him. BT is a hero in my eyes in more than one way. He has triumphed, and even though he fights every day to stay above water, he takes hold of his life and has stepped out on one leg and taken the world by storm.

The little dog Bullet was a real dog, though I changed some things in the story to fit. He was well beloved by everyone in my family. Though he lived only a short time, I hope he will live on in this story forever.

So I hope you enjoy this tale about one little dog that opens the eyes of a hero who feels he has nothing left to give.

Acknowledgments

First off I would like to thank the military past, present, and future for all you do.

Christopher Jon. You once again captured my character perfectly. I told you this was my picture, didn't I?

BT Urruela. Oh hell, for just being you and inspiring me to write this character.

Anya Kelleye, my wonderful and talented cover artist, for designing yet another masterpiece.

A shout out to Chandra Crawford for letting me know I was on point with this story.

Lisa Angel Miller for brainstorming with me when I was stuck.

Anita hell for everything.

Dedication

For all the men and women who fight for our freedom, those that have lost their lives, and those that come home with injuries.

And one incredible dog, Bullet, who will forever hold a special place in my heart. I miss you so much.

Quote

"It doesn't take a hero to order men into battle. It takes a hero to be one of those men who goes into battle." – H. Norman Schwarzkopf, Jr.

PROLOGUE

O ur Humvee jostled and bumped down
the one lane dirt road. As we drove, we
kept an eye out for anything resembling
an insurgent. Two men stepped out from the
cover of an abandoned car, with machine guns
aimed in our direction.

"Watch out!" my lieutenant hollered.
Without stopping I veered our vehicle around
them, their gunfire peppering the front and
sides. My hands gripped the steering wheel as I
tried to maneuver out of the way.

Before I knew it, we made contact with some debris. I tried but failed to control the vehicle, and we ran off the road. Then the tires hit what felt like a roadside bomb. A huge shockwave rolled the Humvee onto its side, throwing me around like a ragdoll. My ears throbbed and the sounds around me were foggy. Glass shattered and the sudden onslaught of heat poured through the broken window suffocated me.

My body was jostled around in the cab of the vehicle. My head bounced off the side a few times, and a headache built up that I was sure wouldn't go away for a long time. The pungent odor of burning plastic stung my nostrils. Through the haze and smoke, pieces of metal flew around me. As the vehicle rolled two or three times, pain stabbed through my leg.

We skidded to a stop on the edge of the road. My hand gripped my knee and the wetness soaked my hand. A strong coppery smell filled the cab. When I glanced down, I saw red blood covering my hand, and a sharp piece of metal sticking out from my leg. I reached back down and grasped it, causing more pain to course through my body.

The smell of burnt rubber caused my nose to run and my eyes to water. Voices screamed out, but I couldn't make out anything coherent. Then silence followed, and the smell of gasoline permeated the inside of the vehicle. *Oh shit*, was all I could think. *I'm going to be burned alive.*

Two hands dragged me from the wreckage. "Hold on, Jackson, we got—"

Before he could finish, the cold metal passed through my leg and darkness clouded my vision. As the pain grew, I heard gunshots and screaming voices all around me.

I woke to a cold needle puncturing my arm as I lay out on the dusty side of the road. The pain surging through my body was numbed by the morphine being pumped through my veins. I tried to move but couldn't.

"How are you feeling, Sergeant Ledet?" a medic asked, cowering close to me. Even though I spoke, no sound came from my dry mouth, which was caked with dirt. "We'll have you out of here as soon as the chopper arrives."

I rolled my head over, not able to say much of anything else. The medic patted me on the shoulder.

"No need to speak."

I drifted into unconsciousness as the morphine took hold of my wits and made everything disappear. The last thing I heard was the whir of a helicopter in the distance.

The continuous beeping of a machine pulled me from unconsciousness and I tried to pry my eyes open. When I opened them, I scanned the room and saw gray walls. The room smelled strongly of antiseptic and death. *Oh shit, I'm dead.*

My thoughts were brought to the edge of my brain. Through the haze, I blinked once. The nurse smiled at me.

"Nurse, how is our patient?" A doctor in scrubs walked over to the side of my bed.

"Still a little groggy."

"Good. Start weaning him off the pain meds slowly; we need to get him started on his rehabilitation."

As I shifted in the bed, the realization that something was wrong hit me like a ton of bricks. I fumbled removing the blanket off of me to see my right leg, or what was left of it, thickly bandaged.

"What the fuck? What happened to my leg?" My voice was hoarse and unrecognizable to me.

A hand settled on my shoulder. "Sergeant, we had to remove it."

"Why?" I cried out.

The doctor pulled a chair over beside me. It scraped against the floor, and my anger, hurt, and other emotions raced through me. My stomach knotted and I began to sweat profusely. I clinched the sheets covering my body in my fists. The machines beeped erratically.

"Because, Sergeant, it was not viable. It couldn't be saved. By the time the gunfire had stopped and we were able to get you here, the leg was barely holding on by a few tendons." My breathing became ragged. The doctor placed his hand on my shoulder. "You need to calm down."

I tried to calm my breathing. Tears flooded my eyes. "What happened?"

He leaned forward. "You don't remember?"

"No." My head barely moved from side to side on the pillow.

"Your vehicle hit an IED, and a piece of shrapnel was embedded in your leg. After they pulled you from the wreckage, you were also shot in the leg."

I tried to roll over but couldn't. My anger consumed me, and I began to hit the bed with my fists. He nodded to the nurse. The sedative coursed coldly through my veins, and soon my eyelids slid shut.

The next day as I lay in bed, a knock sounded on the door. It opened slightly, and one of my unit members looked around.

"Jackson, you up for some visitors?" I nodded slightly. "So how are you feeling buddy?" I glanced over at him and tried to speak, but it was as if my mouth was stuffed with cotton. "It's okay, don't speak. I just wanted to bring you something to remind you that you are a hero." He opened his hand palm up, and a bullet sat in the middle.

"Water," I croaked. The nurse handed me a cup. I sipped the liquid and let it slide down my throat. "What is this?" I choked out.

"It's a symbol of you being our hero."

"I'm no hero." My anger echoed in my voice.

"Yes, you are. They said that if you hadn't maneuvered us out of the way, we'd all be dead. You saved us." He handed the bullet to me. "Maybe the nurse can help you add it to your dog tags and St. Jude medallion."

I gripped the bullet in my hand. "But didn't I hit an IED?"

"You barely missed it, but those things go off if the wind blows the wrong way."

I shook my head and tears slid down my face. "But I lost part of me."

He sighed. "I know, but you are a hero to us all." A few other men from my unit stood behind him. I couldn't take this, so I turned my head away from them.

"Don't worry about him, he's medicated. He has a long road of recovery ahead of him," the nurse said as she adjusted something on my IV.

As they left, they each patted me on my shoulder. "We will be here for you always, Sergeant."

During the next weeks, all I wanted was to be taken from my agony and pain. One morning I woke to the constant beeping of the machines. Today the pain above my stump, unlike other days, was more constant, but as I lay on my back it slowly began to dissipate, though my body began to throb. I figured it was because I'd been doing an hour of PT two to three times a week, as well as having lessons on taking care of what was left of my limb.

6

The door opened, and a nurse walked in. "Good morning, Sergeant Ledet. How are you feeling this morning?"

"Okay," I grumbled.

"Just okay?" she asked, checking my vitals. Her hand touched the bullet pendant around my neck.

"Yes, I'm fine as shit."

She laughed. "Do you kiss your girlfriend with that mouth?" Her hand lingered on the bullet. "What is this?"

The metal felt cool on my skin as it sat beside the medallion from.... My thoughts trailed, and I pushed her hand away. "None of your business." Thoughts of Bex swarmed through me. *Shit, Bex.* I had to get a message to her. "Um, nurse...."

She smiled. "Yes, Sergeant?"

"Could I have a piece of paper and a pen? I need to write a letter to someone."

"Sure thing. I'll be right back. Then it's time for your therapy."

The nurse walked back in with a pad and pen and I took them, my hand shaking. As the ink hit the paper, I made the hardest decision I'd ever faced.

Dear Bex,

It's been awhile. Sorry for that. My life is not my own anymore. I have almost no free time. I think about you and me when I have those precious moments, and I wish I was there.

I hoped to return to your embrace and smell your jasmine scent that covered you from head to toe. Kiss your lips once again. I've been away from you for so many years, none of them a walk in the park.

From the moment we met in high school, I knew you were the one. Do you remember Senior prom? You were so beautiful. We danced the night away. We even danced after we got to the cabin. It was a "best night" for me.

We have a lot of memories at that cabin; cookouts, camping, and fishing. Your family and my family just seemed to merge into one big family. They were always together. You always loved to hike to the old fire tower and then climb up it. We had a lot of fun in that old tower. I remember swimming in the lake for hours, floating with our feet sticking toward the sky, our toes showing above the water.

Do you remember our weekend trip to New Orleans? We rode bikes through the Quarter and walked through all the voodoo shops. You were so freaked out. And I believe that you were a little scared when we toured the graveyards. I piggybacked you almost the entire tour. Those were the best days for me.

I was a different man then...just a kid really. Life here is different, harder. I have come to realize that I am leaving a part of myself in this God forsaken place. Parts of me that I will never get back. Parts of me that you need. The days here are filled with solitude and so much hatred from the enemy. Bombs light up the city, only to cover it with smoke and bring wreckage to all that live here. This place is filled with nothing but death and despair. I've seen so much, lived so much. Every day I've spent *in this desert fighting the good fight, the only thing keeping me alive was knowing I'd see you again one day.*

I took a deep breath; could I do this? I shook my head and muttered to myself, "Yes, it's the right thing to do." A tear slid down my face and my hand shook as I placed the tip of the pen back onto the paper. The ink replaced my thoughts with words.

I'm so sorry. I can't keep you from a life you deserve—one so much better than I can give you. Waiting for me, it's not right. I must let you go. With the recent events that have taken place, I feel in my heart you must move on. I'm no longer the man you desire or should have in your life. I'm broken, half a man, never to be whole again. No longer the man you deserve to take care of you.

Bex, do not be upset with me, this is for the best. I hope you find someone more deserving of your love. I also return this symbol of our love and hope. I know you wished for me to make it out of the godforsaken place and come back to you.

Loving you has been the greatest privilege. It's a gift that I cherish. However, some gifts are temporary. Bex, I love you, I will always love you, but I am no longer a complete man. Parts of me, huge parts of me, are gone. They are not coming back. I am no longer what is best for you. Bex and Jax ends here.

I want you to move on, to live a complete life. I want you to love with your whole heart, live with your whole body, and thrive with your whole soul. Walk, run, dance, swim hike, laugh...LIVE.

I will always love you, but I'm yours no more.

Jax

I removed the small medallion of St. Jude, patron saint of lost causes—but more importantly, of hope and prayer—from the chain around my neck. I folded the letter and dropped the silver pendant inside. Quickly, before I could tear up the letter, I stuffed the paper and its contents into the envelope.

The nurse came in. "Sergeant you have some visitors would you like to see them before you go to therapy?"

"Who?"

"Your parents" A knock resounded on the door. "Come in," the nurse said. The door quickly opened and my mom popped her head around the frame.

"Hey Jax are you up for some more company?"

"Sure mom."

Both my mom and dad walked inside. The expression on my mom's face was sad, the look of pity broke my heart."

I tried to sit up but she placed her hand on my shoulder. "It's okay son don't."

Sighing I settled back into my pillow. "How are you mom and dad?" I asked as I turned my head looking at him. We are good.

"We have a surprise for you?"

"What is it?" I grumbled.

"Bex is here she wants to see you."

I shook my head. "No I don't want to see her."

"Are you sure son?" My mom began ringing her hands. "She misses you and has been as worried about you as much as we have."

"Please I can't not like this." I clenched the letter in my hand rumpling the envelope.

12

"Deborah maybe we should go for now. Let him rest some." My mom sniffed and wiped a tear away then kissed me on the forehead. "We'll be back."

After they left I turned to the nurse. "Please give this to Bex for me." The letter shook in my hand.

"Are you sure?"

"Yes. Please don't let her in." The nurse took the folded paper from my hand and left. Minutes later loud sobbing echoed through my room followed by banging on my door.

"I don't care about your injuries, Jax. Don't leave me." Bex hollered at the door and continued her pounding. Seconds later silence fell and I knew she was gone.

CHAPTER 1

Six months later

Familiarity hit me as the train click-clacked to a stop. Without even opening the window, the smell of the heat and ligustrums crawled through the crack in the glass. *"Last stop, Pleasant Street,"* came over the loudspeaker. The same train station that had taken me away from home and to a military life had brought me back. I sighed deeply as it chugged, finally squealing to a halt. I wiped my forehead and stood up from the leather seat, stretching my leg.

"Young man, would you grab my bag?"

I glanced down and saw a woman. The wrinkles around her eyes gave her a timeless look. "Yes, ma'am." I reached up, balancing on the tiptoe of my good foot, and grabbed her bag. "Here you go, ma'am."

She smiled kindly. "Nice to see some young people still have manners." I nodded. She leaned into me. "Thank you for your service."

"How did you know?"

Her expression held a hint of sorrow. "My husband had the same look on his face when he returned home. Sadness enveloped in a smidge of hope. I promise you, son, it will get better; you just have to be open. Remember you are a hero to so many people."

"Yes, ma'am." I handed her the bag and waved her into the aisle. My heart pounded as I watched her toddle away from me.

Waiting for my turn to exit, I grabbed my duffle bag from the seat beside me. In front of me, a little girl held the hand of her mother as she waited to step off the train. But she stopped and tugged on her mother's hand. "Wait, Mommy, wait."

"What is it, Rebecca?"

"I left Teddy on my seat." She returned to her seat but began crying. The tears poured down her face at what I deduced was the loss of a long time stuffed friend. "Mommy, he's not here."

From the corner of my eye I saw the ear belonging to the brown bear underneath the seat. I reached underneath and pulled it from its hiding spot. When I picked it up, the bullet from around my neck fell from its hiding spot under my shirt. I quickly tucked it back underneath. "Wait, is this what you are missing?"

The little girl turned around. "Thank you, mister."

"You're welcome." I plastered a fake smile on my face.

She took the offered bear and hugged me. As she ran off she exclaimed. "Mommy, Mommy, the nice guy found Teddy." The mother turned around and smiled.

After the people had dispersed, I sighed and decided I finally had to get off the train. My life had inevitably changed, but was it for the good or...?

Descending the metal steps, I hoisted the green army issued bag over my shoulder. The heat hit me as I stepped off the train. I wiped my brow again as sweat beaded across my forehead. I was home, and the reality of my new life sucker punched me in the gut. I had to regain my composure and not run screaming.

Home sweet home, better known as Legacy Falls. It had been about seven years since I had set foot in the small southern town. Granted, I'd come back for holidays when I could. But things were so different now. I repositioned my duffle bag and stepped out away from the train. I glanced around the old fashioned train station looking for my parents.

"Jackson!" I heard the shrill scream from my mother and faked a smile as she waved me over to her. In her hand she held a tiny American flag and waved it in the air. "Welcome home, Jackson."

I walked through the crowd of people, and several of them clasped me on the shoulder. "Thanks for your service."

"You're welcome."

As I made my way through the throngs of people, one woman stopped me and hugged me, with tears brimming in her eyes. I returned the hug and headed over to my family.

"Hey, Mom. How are you?"

She grabbed me in a motherly bear hug. After what felt like an eternity, she pulled back and wiped a tear that slid down her cheek. "You look good. How are you, son? Everything okay with the...?"

"Mom, come on; I'd rather not discuss it." She eyed me and suddenly I stepped back in time to when she'd scolded me. I smiled. "Mom, sorry, but I'd rather not talk about it. Besides, you know I missed you and Dad." I mustered up the best smile I could.

"Wait, what about me?" my sister Suzie asked.

I turned and gazed into the deep brown eyes of my sister. She had grown so much since I'd deployed.

"Suzie, is that you?" I grinned at my little sister. "No way this is my little sister." I glanced over to my mom, then dropped my bag and grabbed my sister in a bear hug.

"Ja...x, I...ca...n't...breathe." She coughed.

I let her go. "Sorry, Suzie."

"It's Susan now. I am twenty and in college."

I ruffled her head. "You'll always be Suzie to me."

She grinned up at me, eyeing me over the top of her sunglasses. "Jackson, does Becki know you are...?"

I grimaced as I saw my mother nudge her. I could only assume my ex had told my mother of our breakup, but for some reason, they hadn't told my sister.

I quickly changed the subject. "So, college huh?"

She eyed me quizzically. "What is going on with you and Bex?"

This time my father interrupted us as he grabbed me in a hug and changed the subject. "So son, let's get you home. I'm sure you are tired from your trip."

"Thanks, Dad...I am."

He wrapped an arm over my shoulder and spoke so only I could hear. "Your mother and sister are just worried about you."

I limped a bit to the car, the effect of sitting for so long and not being able to stretch what was left of my leg. The ride brought home so many memories I almost couldn't take it. As I pushed myself further into the leather seat, a slight pain radiated from my nonexistent calf to my thigh. I remembered in the hospital the doctors had called it phantom pain. I rubbed my leg...or the part of it above my prosthesis. I shook my head then raised my arms over my head, leaning back even more. For a second I closed my eyes and nodded off.

"Pow!"

"What the fuck!" I jumped in my seat, and my eyes popped open. My panic erupted, and my father slammed on the brakes. I flew forward and hit the console.

"Jackson Hamilton Ledet, watch your language!"

"Jeezus, Debra, give him a break. He's been through enough trauma, and I'm sure that car backfiring didn't help."

I saw her turn to my dad and eye him after his use of Jesus. But all he did was laugh, so she turned her attention back to my language. "Yes, but he should watch his words in front of his sister."

"Good gracious, Mom; like I haven't heard that word before," my sister said, exasperated.

I drifted back to sleep as my parents and sister continued bickering. As the car pulled into the driveway, it jostled me awake. I trudged out of the car and headed into the house and up to my old room, ignoring all the chit chat and calls that dinner would be ready soon. To be honest, I didn't really care. I just wanted to crash into my bed and sleep.

I flopped down on the bed, still in my clothes. Once my head hit the pillow, my eyes closed and I fell asleep.

I barely heard the door creak open as my mother tiptoed inside and left a tray of food on my nightstand. "I love you, Jackson." She kissed me on the cheek and left.

CHAPTER

2

Three weeks later

I stretched in my bed and the chatter downstairs fully woke me.

"But Mama, he needs to live again."

"Susan, not now!" my mother exclaimed. "Give him time. He's been through a traumatic event."

"I know, Mother, but he needs to realize it's not the end of the world."

"Susan!" she gasped. "Your brother needs time to heal, and to him, it feels that way."

I rubbed my chin, sat up in bed, and shrugged. *Damn, if only my sister knew the truth. What good am I now, broken?* I threw my one leg over the bed and sighed.

Reaching over, I grabbed the prosthetic and connected it to what was left of my leg. I stood and balanced myself, then shuffled off to the bathroom. Leaning over the sink, I braced my hands on either side and hung my head. A deep sigh escaped my mouth. After a few moments, I turned on the faucet and slid my hands under the cool water, then splashed some onto my face. When I glanced up into the mirror, the reflection staring back at me was unrecognizable. My eyes were red, my beard longer than usual. Shit, I looked like crap. I tugged at the almost full beard. I also needed a shave.

I shook my head. "Damn, how long have I been sleeping?" I sniffed myself and grimaced. "Must have been awhile; I smell like the dead."

"Jackson, breakfast is ready," my mother hollered from her usual perch on the stairs. Quickly I wiped my face with a towel and then flopped the towel over the edge of the sink. After pulling a pair of jeans from the back of the chair beside the door, I stuffed my legs into them. Quickly I shoved a shirt over my head and stalked downstairs. My bare foot slapped on the hardwood floors, and I plastered a smile on my face the second I walked into the kitchen.

"Eggs, or—"

"Coffee."

"Come on, son, you need to eat."

"Debra, let him be, dear. He's a grown man and will eat when he feels like it," my father said without looking away from the paper.

"He may be a grown man, but he's mine to worry about." She turned back to the stove and sighed as I poured myself a cup of the hot black coffee. I let the beverage warm me and remembered when Bex would wrinkle up her nose at me for drinking it black. I nudged all thoughts of Bex from my brain. Not today. I wouldn't think of her.

I sat down, and my dad handed me part of the newspaper. "Here, son."

"Thanks, Dad."

I flipped it open, wondering if anything newsworthy had happened since I'd returned home. I caught my father staring at me over the paper, and knew I was in for a discussion soon. I waited patiently for him to say something, and I didn't have to wait too long. As I put the mug to my mouth again, he spoke.

"Jax, after breakfast, do you think you could help me outside maybe, cleaning out the boat?"

Carefully I placed the mug down and nodded. "Yes."

"Good. After you finish your breakfast," he eyed my mug, "meet me outside."

After about ten minutes, I stood and placed my cup in the sink, patted my mother on the shoulder, and headed outside to help my father…or better yet, hear what was on his mind. I meandered through the yard, where the fresh cut grass invaded my senses. I shaded my eyes from the sun as I headed over to the boat shed. The boat sat in the water bumping up against the sides of the building. "Dad, where are you?"

"Over here, son." I heard his disembodied voice coming from somewhere.

"Where?" I stepped a foot onto the wooden pier that surrounded the boat and looked around inside the boat.

My dad sat there digging into an ice chest. "Come on, Jax. Want a beer?" He offered me a bottle.

I chuckled and took the beer. "Dad, isn't it too early for this?" I took it and popped the cap off.

"Don't tell your mom. Besides, isn't there a song or something about it's always time for beer?"

I laughed. "Do you mean 'It's Five O'clock Somewhere'?"

"I guess so." He looked off into the distance. "Son, what's going on?"

"Nothing like beating around the bush, huh Dad."

He looked off onto the lake behind our house. "Jax, life is too short. You more than anyone can understand that."

"I do, Dad."

He turned to face me with an unreadable expression. "Then what is going on with you? Why would you do what you did to Becki?"

"Dad, you wouldn't understand."

"Why don't you try me?" He eyed me over the glasses sitting on the bridge of his nose.

I shook my head. "I can't."

He sighed deeply. "Well, you need to do something; you need to live your life. Just because you lost a leg doesn't mean you can give up. Besides, your mother won't admit it, but she's worried about you."

"Dad, first of all, I'm living my life. As for Bex, she deserves someone else." As the words came out I tried to believe what I said. But deep down it was for the best. I couldn't let her live a life with someone that was half a man.

He shook his head and chugged his beer. "No, you aren't. What you're doing is sleeping your life away. And Bex? She loves you. Did you know what you did hurt her immensely?" I shook my head, my heart heavy at the realization I'd hurt her so much. But my head told me it was for the best. He continued without looking at me, his voice laced with sadness. "She would visit your mother and cry her eyes out about that damn letter."

25

I grumbled. "You don't know what I went through."

"No I don't, but I do know my son, and he is a strong man. One that doesn't sleep his life away. One that doesn't throw a girl like Bex away." He looked up at me. "Son, she could help you through the hard times." I shrugged and he changed the subject. "You need to get out of the house."

"What do you propose?" I inquired.

"I don't know…go volunteer somewhere. Why not go over to the local vet clinic? You use to love helping out there when you were young." He grinned at me. "I know Dr. Hutchinson could use some help at the clinic."

I finished off my beer and stood. "I don't really feel like it."

"Jax, Doc is a good man, and he is also a veteran like you. Maybe he could knock some sense into you."

"Dad, he has no idea what I'm going through."

He shook his head. "Maybe not, but you know as well as anyone what animals can do for people. That's all I meant, son."

A deep sigh escaped me as I started to walk away. "Dad, if you insist I will go and help."

My dad stood, walked over to me, and grabbed me by the shoulders. "No son, you need to do it for you, not me. Just because you lost a leg doesn't mean you get to throw away your life."

I moaned. "You have no idea what I've lost."

His grip grew firmer on my shoulders and a look of determination flashed in his eyes, "No, but I will not lose my son. Please think about it."

"I will," I lied.

CHAPTER

3

Sluggishly I headed back to the house, stuffing my hands in my pockets. A dozen or so thoughts swam around my brain. Even though I'd never admit it, my father was right. I had to get past my injury and live again. This in no way meant I wanted a relationship with Bex, or anyone else for that matter. Especially since I was no longer whole. But I did need to come back to the living and stop shuffling through the days in my present zombie state. I figured it would be wise to take my father's advice; well, after I showered. I sniffed myself again. *Holy shit, I smell.* Sighing deeply, I headed through the house and upstairs.

"Honey, did everything go okay with your father?" my mother asked, poking her head around the doorframe of the kitchen.

I stopped on the stairs and nodded my head. "Yes, Mom."

"Good. Where are ya headed?"

Not really wanting the third degree from my mom, I said simply, "I'm headed to go visit Doc."

She grinned before popping back into the kitchen. "Good. It will do you good to get out of the house."

I chuckled lightly and continued up the staircase.

An hour later, refreshed, I grabbed my keys to the old pickup. "I'll be back later, Mom," I yelled. Her reply was inaudible as I stepped outside.

Heading down the pathway to the old beater, my foot caught a hole and I tripped and fell. "Fuck," I hollered as loud as I could, not caring who heard me. I pushed myself up and dusted my hands off on my jeans, then continued to the truck.

I scooted inside and turned the ignition. The truck hiccupped and popped a couple of times, but sputtered off. With the key still in I turned it again, this time gunning the engine. As it purred to life, I slammed my palm down on the steering wheel. *Damn, I wonder if Dad even started it while I was gone.*

Backing up, I maneuvered the vehicle down the driveway and headed into town. The trip down the two-lane highway was short. On the way, I saw glimpses of southern gulf living. People passed me headed away from town with their boats hooked to the back of pickup trucks, presumably on the way to do some fishing. I grinned and thought I should take the boat out next weekend.

Thoughts of Bex once again plagued me. Her in that teeny tiny bikini giving me a run for my money when it came to catching fish. I shook my head, emphatically trying to dislodge the memories.

I turned my attention to the trees and bodies of water as I headed into town. As I drove down the two lane highway the land changed drastically, and cows peppered the green grass like little black and white dots. I took a left at the intersection into town and passed my old high school. By the looks of it, things hadn't changed with the football team out for practice.

Fond memories played like a movie reel in my head. I pulled over for a second and replayed my high school days; me on the field and Bex up in the stadium watching me from over the pages of whatever novel she was reading at the time. She would wave at me when I looked up. Then she would blow me a kiss and delve back into whatever story had her mind captivated. Jealousy was never a problem with me, since I knew I captivated her heart.

I turned my attention back to the young men on the field and sighed. These people didn't know how lucky they had it with guys like me fighting for their freedom. I slammed my hand on the steering wheel and tried hard not to let my feelings get the better of me. *Shit*! Next thing I would be laying down on the sofa telling my darkest secrets to some damn shrink. And that wasn't about to happen anytime soon.

A few more turns and I pulled into the parking spot in front of the vet clinic and shrugged my shoulders. "All right, Jackson. Get this over with so you can move on and get everyone off your damn back."

My hands shook a bit nervously. I mean hell, I'd forbidden my parents to tell anyone I was back. I really didn't want people making a fuss over me. So before my father had his little talk with me, I had planned on laying low for some time.

As I opened the truck door, it creaked. After taking a deep breath, I slid out. Slamming the door, I slid a hand down my chin and mentally told myself, *Come on, Jackson, you can do this. After all, it's just Doc.*

I planted one foot in front of my fake one and made my way to the door of the clinic. I pushed the door open, and a barrage of yips and barks met me. As I entered, the strong scent of cleaner mixed with a slight urine and feces smell assaulted my nostrils.

I walked inside and was greeted by a friendly looking older woman. "Yes, may I help you, young man?"

I nodded. "Is Doc in?"

She smiled. "Yes. Can I tell him who is here to see him?"

"Yes ma'am, Jackson Ledet."

She smiled again and nudged her glasses back onto her nose. "Wait right here."

I stuffed my hands into the pockets of my jeans and paced back and forth, wearing a path in the linoleum.

"How the hell are you, Jax?"

I turned around and saw the vet that I had volunteered for when I was young staring at me. "I could be better, sir."

"When did you get back?"

I drew a blank, since most of my time had been spent in bed. "Hmm...maybe a couple of weeks ago."

Doc walked over to me and shook my hand, then placed his arm over my shoulder. The lady walked around and sat back at her desk. "Milly, I'd like to introduce you to a hero of this town. This here is an old family friend, back from overseas. Sergeant Jackson Hamilton Ledet."

I hung my head at the apparent adoration from the old man.

"It's nice to meet you, Jackson." She stood and walked over to me, offered me her hand, then hugged me. When she let go, she patted me on the forearm and turned to Doc. "Now Doc, don't embarrass the poor kid." Then she smiled at me.

"Come on, Jackson, follow me. So, how can I help you?"

As I followed him to the back, I turned and smiled back at Milly, mouthing, "Thank you."

"You are welcome," she mouthed back, then returned to sit behind the desk.

"I was wondering, Doc, if you needed any help around here?"

He walked into a room that smelled strongly of antiseptic and shuffled some papers around before he spoke. "As a matter of fact, we could use some help. We are down a dog walker. Would that be okay for now?"

I nodded. "Of course; I could walk the dogs."

"Good." He walked around to me and placed his hands on my shoulders. "Heard about your accident son. I'm sorry, Jackson."

I shrugged. "It is what it is. Wait...how did...? Never mind. Dad, huh?"

He chuckled, removed his glasses, and wiped the lenses. "Son, the whole town knows." He placed the glasses back on the bridge of his nose, and his expression changed to empathy. "Jackson, you know you can talk to me about anything."

I nodded.

"I'm here for you. As you know, I still have a bit of shrapnel in my ass." He laughed.

"Doctor Hutchinson, stop telling those fibs about your backside." We laughed as Milly hollered from the front.

"I swear that woman has the hearing of a bat," he whispered to me.

"I heard that." The rest of her words were incoherent.

I laughed at the thought that Doc hadn't changed in the years I'd been gone, which for me was good to know. Changing the subject, I leaned on the table, shifting my weight on my legs. "So, what can I start on?"

"There are a few dogs that need some attention. Why don't you head out to the kennels? I think they may need you as much as you need them. So many unwanted pets in the world," he replied sadly, returning to his stack of papers.

I nodded. "I think I've heard that from someone else today."

He looked up at me and smiled. "Your dad is a smart man, Jax." He winked at me.

"It doesn't surprise me how much you and my father are alike." I turned away and headed off to the kennels. "Thanks, Doc." I hollered back at him.

"No problem. If you want, you can show up tomorrow. I'm a little short staffed here in the vet clinic as well," I heard him say as I walked out.

The closer I got to the room containing the boarded dogs and cats, the louder the barking got. When I entered the kennel room, I was bombarded by barking and whining.

"Hold on, guys and girls. I'll get you all walked." I pulled a leash off the hook on the wall and started with the first dog. "Come on boy, you ready to take a walk?"

The dog wagged his tail in response and I clipped the leash onto his collar. One after the other I walked the dogs. The yard in the back was fenced in, so I let them off the leash to do their business. I figured if I didn't want someone standing over me while I peed, the dogs would appreciate it if I gave them the same respect.

After I'd walked the last dog, I hung the leash back up and headed through the building, the smells and sounds reminiscent of my childhood. Finally I couldn't take it anymore; I headed outside, telling myself I would be back tomorrow.

CHAPTER 4

   The next morning I woke and shuffled out of bed earlier than anyone else in the house. I plugged in the old fashioned coffee maker and dropped my head as I waited for it to percolate. I chuckled at the fact that Mom refused to change with the times. As the coffee bubbled in the pot, the scent of chicory lifted up and started to wake me.

   After a quick breakfast, I headed back to Dr. Hutchinson's Vet Clinic. When I walked inside it was awfully quiet. Milly greeted me with a smile.

She covered the receiver with her hand and whispered, "Doc's in the back."

"Thanks, Milly."

When I entered the back, I saw Doc deep in thought as he bent over a cat. He hummed some old war song, which I knew from experience meant he'd had a bad night. The old vet had been wounded in the Vietnam War, though he never really told us the truth of his injury; hence the shrapnel in the ass story everyone got.

I stood in the doorway, not wanting to disturb him, and waited patiently for him to notice me. He looked up at me and waved me inside. Then he filled a syringe with the drug that would help the cat sleep through its surgery. When the needle stuck the cat, she meowed and hissed in anger and protest. It took a couple of minutes for the drugs to take effect.

"Wanna help me prep this cat for surgery?"

"Sure thing, Doc." I walked around, pulled the ropes from the hook on the table, and began tying a slip knot to each leg, then wrapped each one around the four corners of the table. Once all four appendages were spread I picked up the clippers. When I turned them on, the purr of the motor came to life. With quick movements I shaved the feline's belly. After I washed it with antibacterial soap, I looked around the room for the spray bottle of blue stuff we sprayed on the animal. "Doc, where is the blue spray?"

He pointed to the shelf behind me. "Oh, I moved the chlorhexidine to the second shelf."

I grabbed the bottle and sprayed the cat, then poured a little alcohol over the animal's abdomen. After I'd finished prepping the cat, I picked up a clean blue drape, unfolded it, and draped it over the animal.

"All done, Doc." I petted the cat's head and stepped out of the way.

He smiled. "Just like old times." He grinned at me. "It's like riding a bike."

"Yes, sir."

"Thank you, Jackson."

"Anytime."

"You oughta consider coming to work for me full time, not on a volunteer basis. I could get you some classes for veterinary technician."

"I'll think about it, sir." He nodded and turned his attention back to the cat. "So, would you like for me to feed and walk the dogs?"

He nodded. "Please. Then I'll need you to bring me the hound puppy in kennel number four, but don't feed him. He's being adopted and needs to be neutered."

"Okay."

I smiled at Doc, knowing the people were getting a deal from him. He had a heart of gold when it came to the animals he cared for, which sometimes meant being taken advantage of, but I doubted he'd ever change. The old man loved animals and wanted the best for them. He'd taken the veterinary oath to the tenth degree.

He always did his best when it came to treating those who came into his clinic. He was also known for the old ways of medicine; he was a man of the past, not using many updated tricks of the trade, so to speak. His main focus was on the animal and their owner. Money was important but not at the expense of the animal. He catered to those with little funds. He was known to take in a dog or two at times and find them homes.

I entered the kennel room and a barrage of barks and meows met me. When I walked down the narrow stretch between the kennels, the dogs began barking and howling even louder. "Hold on guys, one at a time." I chuckled at the dogs bounding and leaping at the kennel doors. They looked as if they were doing a three-year-old's version of the pee pee dance, only on four legs. I glanced around and noticed a couple of empty cages. One or two were gone. They must have gotten better and returned home with their owners.

After I had put the last dog back in his kennel, I leashed the hound, walked him inside, and handed him off to Doc. "Before you go, could you bring the cat to recovery?"

"Sure." I gently took the offered cat, careful not to let his head hang, and walked down the hall to the recovery room. Juggling the cat in my arms and opening the cage, I placed him on a blanket and positioned him so he'd be comfortable once he woke.

Afterward, I returned up front. Milly was on the phone, and she looked distressed.

"Hold on, ma'am, don't do anything drastic." Concern bounced off the old woman like a ping pong ball. She eyed me and held her hand up, halting me from leaving. "I'll send someone over to get him now."

I watched with anticipation as she jotted down an address and hung up the phone. "What's going on?"

"Jackson, could you do me a favor?"

"Sure."

She wrung her hands with worry. "That call was from a lady saying this puppy just showed up at her house, and she was afraid her husband was going to put a bullet in his head." As she sat there, tears brimmed at the corners of her eyes. She waved the Post-it note in the air. "Why are people so mean to innocent creatures?" she mumbled to herself.

"Sure, hand me the address." She wiped her eyes and handed me the little yellow piece of paper. "I'll be right back."

She smiled. "Thank you. It's just that some people...." She stuttered. "I mean, it's a defenseless animal."

"I know. Don't worry, I'll be back soon." I tried to calm her as I took the little yellow sticky.

The stifling heat hit me as I opened the door and stepped outside. "Damn, who opened the gates of hell?" I muttered as I made my way to my truck. Once inside I sighed, hoping nothing bad happened to that little puppy.

I glanced down at the yellow sticky and read the address, then shook my head. I knew this area, and it wasn't the safest one. The place was littered with trash, and most of the people that lived out there didn't take kindly to people trespassing.

I drove the fifteen miles to the address and stopped my truck outside of a run-down shack. The roof hung on by a single beam. The littered yard contained rusty metal drums and rolls of old wire. A dilapidated old truck sat perched in the distance, carrying only one rotted out tire.

Carefully I exited my truck; years of training had me on high alert. *Never can be too careful, especially if someone thinks you are trespassing.* I stepped out into ankle-deep grass, but in some areas it was knee-deep. *Damn, I hope there aren't hidden animal traps in all this mess. That's one thing I wouldn't be surprised to find out here.*

When I got closer to the house, the screen door creaked open. "Who's there?"

I held my hands up, showing that I meant no harm. "Hi, ma'am, I'm from the vet clinic."

An old woman with a face that told of a hard and troubled life peeked around the broken screen door. She stepped outside but stopped inches over the threshold, her hand holding onto what was left of the wooden frame of the door. "Who are you?"

"I'm from the vet clinic, the one you called, ma'am," I repeated.

She shuffled out further onto the planked porch in moth-eaten slippers. The stains on the fuzzy white slippers resembled coffee...my better guess was chewing tobacco. She stopped at the railing, her hand gripping the skinny piece of wood hanging on by a splinter to the rotten wood steps. In her arms she held a small black and brown puppy. She hobbled down one of the steps, careful not to step in the gaping holes on them.

"Are ya here to get him?"

"Yes, ma'am."

"I'm so sorry to cause a ruckus, but my husband doesn't like no dogs on the land."

"No worries, ma'am; we'll take good care of him."

I headed off the porch to go to my truck. She held onto the railing, which looked like at any moment it would crumble into pieces. She placed the puppy in my arms and hobbled back up the rickety steps.

"Now you best be hurrying before you're found here."

"Yes, ma'am."

I quickened my pace, but she'd spoken too late. I turned around as a beat-up old truck flew into the driveway, throwing gravel everywhere.

It swerved, barely missing my truck. One rock hit my windshield and a star shaped crack held firm in the glass. The truck spun its tires in the gravel and grass, and rumbled to a stop within inches of mine.

The door flew open, and a huge behemoth of a man tumbled out. If I hadn't been worried about being shot, I would have chuckled at the sight of what resembled Humpty Dumpty exiting the vehicle.

"What's goin' on here?" he growled. His belly flopped so far over I was sure his feet hadn't seen daylight in God knew how long.

I backed up, never taking my eye off the man. "Sorry, sir, I was just leaving."

He eyed me and pulled a gun off the gun rack attached to the back window of his truck. "You sure about that?" He aimed the gun at me and cocked it.

I kept backing up towards my truck slowly. "Yes, sir, I was just leaving. No need to fire the gun, sir."

"I won't be firing unless you don't get off my land. What are you doing here?"

"Nothing, sir. I made a wrong turn and needed directions." I held the puppy close to me, away from the man's wandering eye.

He kept the barrel of the gun aimed as I opened the door to my beater. "You better git, and don't come back."

"Yes, sir," I nodded, and the puppy burrowed into my arms. Once I got to the truck

I placed him on the seat and slid in beside him. "Come on, little fella. Let's get you somewhere safe." The key slipped into the ignition and this time, the old truck didn't disappoint me.

He yipped in agreement and curled up beside me.

The drive back to town was long and silent. I pulled into the parking spot and looked at the sleeping puppy. "Ready, little fella? We gotta get ya checked out."

He looked up at me, yawned, and flopped his head back down. His long floppy ears drooped on either side of his head. I chuckled, scooped him up, and carried him inside.

The moment I stepped inside Milly came running over to me. "Oh, thank goodness you got him. Is it a him?"

"I don't know...I really didn't look." I laughed. She took the puppy from my arms. I decided not to tell her about the man and the gun. Best not to worry her anymore than need be. Her eyes fell over to his leg. "What's wrong?"

"Oh, nothing. I'm sure everything's fine."

I hadn't noticed his leg before, but then again, I had been too busy escaping from a rabid man with a gun.

"Let's get a good look at ya." She headed to the back with him, and I sat and rubbed the sharp pain in my thigh. Maybe my prosthesis was rubbing on something.

As I sat in the metal chair feeling sorry for myself, the door opened. I never looked up, but a familiar scent of jasmine wafted over to me. I didn't dare look up for fear of who'd entered.

"Miss Milly, are you here?"

"In the back, dear."

I hid my face but saw the shoes in my vision stop.

"Oh, hell no!"

I shook my head and looked up into the face of my ex-fiancée. "Hello, Bex."

"No, you don't get to call me that anymore."

I hung my head in shame. "Bex, I'm sorry."

She stomped away from me and turned, then pointed at me, her anger evident on her face. Damn, that woman was sexy as hell when she was mad.

"You do not get to say that either." She enunciated each word with loathing, which I didn't blame her for.

As soon as she left, I stood and made a run for it.

"Leaving so soon, Jackson?" Milly came out of the back with the puppy, a smile on her face.

I nodded. "Yes, I'll be back tomorrow."

She grinned. "You know Rebecca will be here as well." She winked at me. "She's been helping Doc with the dogs while she's going back to school."

"Damn, I had no idea she worked here."

She laughed. "You never asked."

"Well, maybe tomorrow she won't be so angry." Cowardly I know, but I was not in the mood for another encounter.

"I doubt that."

"Yeah," I mumbled. "I'll see ya tomorrow."

"Are you sure you don't want to foster the—?"

I let the door slam before the rest of her question was out.

CHAPTER

5

When I pulled into the drive at home, a familiar 4x4 belonging to my best friend, Ben, sat in the driveway. I hit my head on the steering wheel. "Damn, I really don't have time for this," I muttered to myself.

As I pondered the idea of putting the truck in gear and backing up, I figured the inevitable time to say hi to my best friend was upon me. I slid out of my truck and ambled up the walkway. As my hand went to grip the knob, the door swung open.

"Well, hey there, Jax."

"Hey, Ben."

"Hey, buddy...so it's true you are home?"

I nodded. "Yeah. Look, I'm sorry I didn't tell you."

"I understand...no hard feelings." He slapped me on the back. "I'm glad you are back."

"So what's up?" I asked, leaning against the doorframe.

"First things first; why did I have to hear from your mom that you were back in town? And weeks later, too?" He eyed me, trying to hide the hurt he felt.

"Damn Ben. I'm sorry." I shrugged my shoulders. "I really have no excuse for not letting you know."

He placed his arm around my shoulder. "Damn, Jax, I can't be mad at you. Though as your best friend I wish you'd told me."

"I know." I grimaced.

"Anyway Jax, I was wondering if you wanted to go and get a beer and play a game of pool."

I sighed.

"Jackson why don't you get out of the house?" my mother hollered from inside the house. I knew this was her doing, her loving way of pushing me to get a life.

I chuckled. "Why the hell not? I could use some money." I slapped Ben on the shoulder. "You got your wallet on ya, huh?" I grinned wide.

He grimaced. "Sure."

I leaned inside the door. "Bye, I'll be back later."

I shut the door, and her voice echoed through the hall. "Have fun."

Ben grinned like the Cheshire cat. "Let's go, Jackson."

"Where are we going?"

"The place we used to drink a beer out back when we couldn't get in. I'm sure you missed the place."

I laughed. "Perfect, because what I need to do is get drunk, actually. And this time we can go inside."

He pushed me down the walkway. "Well, that I think we can accomplish."

We pulled up to the bar, and as the truck pulled to a stop, I glanced out the window. The familiar tree shaped sign that hung over the doorway read Cypress Lounge, established in 1913. I opened the door and stepped out. Shifting my half, a leg a bit, I steadied myself and followed Ben through the door of the smoky, low-lit favorite hangout. The smell of alcohol and cigarette smoke assailed my senses.

"Hey, Ben, I'll get us some drinks. Go find us a table."

He nodded and headed in the direction of the pool tables. I walked up to the bar. "Hey bartender, I need two beers," I said as I dug into my wallet.

The bartender looked up. "Hey, Jackson. How the hell are ya? It's been forever."

"Yes, years." I leaned on the bar. "Jude, how the hell have you been?"

"Pretty good. Took over the bar from the old man about two years ago."

I chuckled. "Damn, do you remember when we used to sneak in here?"

He nodded. "Yes, I do. Got my ass beat a couple of times when my dad found out." He slid a beer toward me. "Glad to see you back home. Sorry to hear about—"

I shook my head, stopping his sentence from being finished. I chugged the drink and wiped my mouth. "It's okay to be back." The liquid flowed through my body like a well-deserved treat.

Ben walked over and slapped his credit card down. "Run me a tab."

Jude laughed. "Hell no! Ben, you know we can't run you a tab."

"Why not?" he grinned.

"Because you never pay."

I laughed. "Still, Ben? Damn it." I turned back to face the bartender. "I got this, Jude." He wiped his hand on a towel and took my offered card. "Keep 'em coming."

"I don't know what the hell Jude is talking about." Ben picked up his beer and headed over to an empty pool table.

"Yeah, sure. Same ole Ben. Though you know we aren't kids anymore." I followed and

50

watched the eyes of everyone following us as we walked through the crowd. At the table, I put my beer down, grabbed my cue, and stood there. "Ben, you can break 'em." He nodded, placed the balls in the rack, and positioned them...after what felt like an eternity. "Come on, bro, hit them before my beer gets warm."

He eyed me, and then with a crack of his cue the balls scattered across the table. "How's that, buddy?"

"Took you long enough," I laughed. On my first shot I knocked a solid into the corner pocket; two more shots and I missed. "Your turn."

I was leaning up against the wall waiting for Ben to miss another shot when a waitress walked up. "Would you like another drink?"

"Another beer." I held up my empty bottle.

"Sure thing, sugar," she drawled out, then turned around and headed back to the bar, sashaying her ass.

"Well, fuck!" I heard Ben exclaim after he missed his shot.

"Okay, Ben, you ready to get your ass handed to you?" I smiled, chalked my cue, and one after the other hit the remaining balls into the pockets. "And that's how ya do it."

As I was about to break for another game, two guys walked up. "Well, well, if it's not Sergeant Jackson Ledet. Care to play against us?"

I eyed them both. "Do I know you?" They didn't answer so I took a gulp from my bottle. "Why not? You up for it, Ben?" I chugged the rest of the beer and slammed the bottle down on a nearby table.

"Sure thing; why not?"

One of the men looked familiar, though I couldn't place him. He smiled and grabbed two cues. Ben nudged me. "Why don't you break, Jax?"

I smiled. "Sure."

As I chalked my cue, I walked around, bent over, and made the shot. The yellow striped ball went into the side pocket. After a few more shots had gone into the pockets, I felt the need for another beer.

One of the guys looked over at me. "So, how are you doing, Jackson?"

I brought the bottle away from my mouth. "Why do you want to know?"

"No reason. I heard you had come back home."

I eyed him and repeated my previous question. "Do I know you?"

He chuckled. "Not me, but you and my brother were in the same unit." He leaned back against the wall and became cocky. "He said you were a bit of a hot head and a know-it-all over there. Ain't that right, Jimmy?"

He nodded his head over to his friend, who was about to hit a ball off the side of the table. The guy stood up and cracked his knuckles. I turned back and faced the little punk in front of me. Then it hit me who this guy was. The similarity to his douchebag brother was uncanny. The same smart ass mouth, the same build. His brother was a guy who had taken an instant dislike to me the moment my feet hit the sands in Iraq. We had gone to rival high schools, and he held on to that rivalry after we left school.

I leaned in closer, inches from his face, and whispered, "I think you have it backwards; your brother was an asshole."

"Don't you talk about my brother."

"Why, does the truth hurt?" I spat.

He held the cue in his hand, his knuckles going white. Then he grinned maliciously at me. "I heard you lost a leg in the war. That it was all your fault too; almost got the men killed."

I reached up and gripped the bullet around my neck. "More lies from that fucking porchdick of a brother of yours."

Anger consumed me, and I stalked over to the bar without a word. When I came back, I had a glass of whiskey in my hand.

Ben grabbed me by the shoulder, but I shrugged his hand off. "Hey Jackson, what's wrong with you?" Ben asked.

"Nothing," I said as a waitress came by with a tray full of shots and another glass of whiskey for me. "Keep 'em coming, sugar."

Ben eyed me. "I think you need to slow down."

"I think you need to keep your fucking mouth shut and your head in the game."

Ben shrugged his shoulders as I turned to look at the two guys. "So, how is Connor?"

"Well, he has both of his legs," he said defiantly.

"Look, man, what is your problem?" I asked. I took a swig of my whiskey and slammed down the glass.

"Nothing. I just don't like you."

I eyed him. "Well, the feeling is mutual; you are more like your brother. Now if you want to play, then play, because I am trying my damnedest to get drunk off my ass."

"Jackson," Ben said.

My body built up with anger as I turned on my friend. "Ben, don't. This asshole's brother was a giant dick, and I don't have time for his bullshit. Now he's standing here in front of me telling me it's my fault I lost a leg." I picked up another shot from the ones lined up along the table, slamming it back down.

"I don't have time for this shit," the porchdick's brother retorted.

"Why not, afraid a freak could beat you?"

He glared at me. "No, I just don't think it's a fair fight. You being handicapped and all."

"You fucking asshole." I grabbed his shirt, and he turned around and punched me in the mouth. I felt the warmth from the blood as it dripped down, landing on the floor. Spitting some of it out, I punched him in the gut. He bent over, ran at me, and knocked me to the floor. I kicked him off me. My breathing ragged, I rolled over, braced my hands on the floor, and stood up. "You know, you are a piece of shit." Before I knew it, he stood back up and threw another punch, but I quickly returned it, causing his head to snap backwards. He reached up, punched me in the face, and knocked my prosthesis out from under me. My eye began to swell instantly.

He stood over me. "My brother will be proud of me for besting you, asshole."

I stood back up and dusted myself off. "You want a fight?" I grabbed the pool stick and held it, aiming it at his head. When I swung it, the guy ducked. Voices clamored, and screams about calling the police echoed throughout the bar.

"Jackson, why don't we get out of here?" Ben insisted.

"No, I'm going to do to this guy what I should have done to his brother."

"What the hell...is...?"

I turned around to see Bex standing there, her mouth opened in shock.

CHAPTER 6

Bex turned away from me. "Wait!" As I ran after her, I tripped over something and fell flat on my face.

"No Jax, you are drunk."

"I'm not drunk, but I've sure as hell got a damn good buzz going."

When I looked up, I saw the guy with his arms folded against his chest, grinning down at me. I refocused my attention on Bex, vowing to get revenge on the douchebag who'd tripped me. I tried to get up as Bex had her back to me.

"I knew I'd done the right thing letting you go."

She turned to face me, her face red with anger. "What did you say?" She spoke each syllable carefully.

I stood and wiped my hands down my jeans. I reached for another shot, and the warm liquid slid down my throat. I wiped my mouth and stared at her. "I knew you...would...you know what? Never mind." I turned my back on her and heard her softly cry.

Ben looked at me as I put the cue up and took another swig of my whiskey. "Are you ready, Jackson?"

"Yes, there is nothing here for me."

As I walked past Bex, my face made contact with the floor. I felt arms scoop me up, and on one side of me I could smell the jasmine wash Bex wore. I stumbled as she and Ben walked me to the truck. Ben shoved me in and the door closed. I leaned close to the door and wanted to die even more than before.

From outside the truck, I heard hushed whispers. "Ben, do you mind dropping me off at my house? My friends still want to hang out, and I want to go home."

"Not at all, Becki."

I turned to Bex, and her expression held dozens of emotions, mainly pain and hurt. My head felt foggy and I faced the window again, wishing none of this had happened to me...to us. "Bex...not a whole man, my leg...." I nodded off.

"Jackson, what do you mean?"

"I'm less...."

"Jackson?"

"No leg, less man. You need a whole man...." I drifted off to sleep.

I barely felt Ben hoist me up and drag me to the house. My feet tugged on the ground and I felt the sensation to hurl. "Wait, Ben, I am going to throw up."

"No, you won't."

I inhaled and the soft scent of jasmine flowed around me. I tried to look around but my eye was swollen shut. Ben helped me inside the house and I stumbled up the stairs to my room.

"I'm sorry, Mrs. Ledet," I heard Ben tell my mother.

"It's quite all right; he's been troubled ever since the accident."

"He just needs time for his soul to heal," I heard Ben say.

"Thank you for bringing him home."

Once I got into my room I flopped down on my bed, my legs sprawled across it. I didn't even bother to remove my fake one. My back was pressed against the mattress. Once again I smelled jasmine and swore I heard the soft shuffle of feet as I drifted off to sleep. The inner turmoil weighed on my soul in a way that crippled my ability to fully live.

CHAPTER

7

The next morning, I woke to a jackhammer pounding inside my head. "Oh fuck." But there was something else...soft snores. I tried to pry my swollen eye open and saw her; Bex, curled up in a chair across from my bed, a blanket tossed over her, the toes of her white socks peeking out. Her toffee-colored hair was splayed over the arm of the chair. I wiped my eyes, trying to see her better. *Shit, this isn't good. Why is she here?*

She stirred and I instantly held my breath. Glancing over to the nightstand to check my phone, I caught a glance of my mother's tonic for hangovers. I sucked it all down and tried my best not to vomit.

"Good, you're awake." I heard Bex's soft just-woke-up voice.

I rubbed my leg and sat up. "Yes. Umm...yeah, I'm up."

She stretched then looked over at me, her blue-green eyes boring holes into me. "Do you want to tell me what that was last night?"

I shook my head. "No. Nothing; I was drunk."

"Jax, you've never gotten so drunk that you started a fight." She sat up and the blanket fell to the floor. Her breasts heaved under her shirt as she took a deep breath.

My brain pounded inside my head. "Bex, why...are you really here?" I stammered.

She sat back in the chair and sighed. "Because I want to know why."

"Why what?" I knew the answer to my question already.

"Why did you write me a Dear Jane letter?" She looked over at me, her face softening but full of hurt. "And I want the truth."

I rubbed my face and sighed as I glanced down at my knuckles. They were bruised, and dried blood remained on them. "Bex, you need a man who is not me."

Her face turned a bright red and her eyes squinted. "I do not want to hear that bullshit anymore."

"Well, it's true." I scooted to the edge of the bed and slipped my pants down, showing my prosthesis. I sat down after pulling my pants back up. "Do you really want a man who has one leg?"

She straightened up and dropped her legs from the chair. Her expression was unreadable as she stood. "Jax, all I ever wanted was you. Why do you not trust me and my heart?"

"No, you deserve someone else." I shook my head.

She walked over and knelt down in front of me. As she pulled something from her pocket, a tear slid down her cheek. My instincts told me to wipe it away, to grab her in my arms, to make love to her, but I couldn't. I stiffened at her close proximity to me. Her jasmine scent floated around me and I almost grabbed her in my arms. The little pendant dangled from a chain.

"I hope you will take this back and remember the love we shared, the hope of a life together." She placed the medallion beside me on the bed. With her hands placed on my knee, her eyes red and moist from tears, she glanced up at me. "Jax, I've loved you since the first time I saw you that day out by the river."

The memories of our first encounter hit me like a tsunami.

***

A bunch of us had gone down to the river on a hot summer day. We were swinging from old tire swings and flipping into the warm water. I had landed in the water after doing a double somersault off the cliff. When I looked up and wiped the water from my face, I saw her, her long toffee hair tied into a ponytail. But the only thing I really remembered was the smile etched on her face, not to mention the two-piece bikini that she sported. It showed off all the right things, the things I wanted my hands all over. At that instant, I knew I wanted....

I shook my head and dislodged the memory. "Bex, you should go. I have a headache."

"Jax, I wish you would trust in our love, trust in me." She gripped my knee and I turned away from her.

"I can't. You deserve someone else."

"I deserve you, Jax." She choked out the words and sniffed.

"I thought after all this time you would have found someone else."

"There is no one else. But to be honest, I'm tired of waiting for you to wake up and see the truth of what's really in front of you."

I kept silent as she pushed herself from the floor. Wiping away a stray tear, she left without another word, shutting the door behind her. As the door slammed, I scoffed. "She'll get over me soon," and drifted back to sleep.

CHAPTER

8

After a few hours, I rolled over, stretched, and groaned. "Damn, what time is it?" My headache still banged and pounded around in my head. I wanted to throw up, I wanted to die. What in the hell was I doing?

"Jax, wake up." My mother knocked on the door and opened it.

"I'm up, Mother."

She walked in and placed her hands on her hips. Well shit...she had that I'm your mother and you will listen to me look. "You know, I figured that once you returned home you would realize what a mistake it was sending Becki that letter. But son, you are a damned fool." I'd never heard my mother curse. "I'd hoped you would wake up and realize you were wrong."

I sighed deeply and shoved the pillow over my face. "Mom, look, I'll be late to the clinic."

"You're already late, son; it's almost noon."

I sat up and rubbed my head. "Damn, Mom."

"Do not use that language in my house."

"Sorry, Mom." I looked at her; she was pissed. The last time she'd worn that expression on her face I'd been out with Ben and we'd been up to our unusual hijinks as kids.

"Before you leave I'll tell you that you are plain stupid, and I'm surprised that my son would let the one girl that no matter what would stand by his side go."

Anger erupted inside me, but at the look on my mother's face, I squelched all ideas to be pissy at her. I ran a hand over my head, then rubbed my beard.

"Mom, I really need to go."

She pointed a finger at me. "Fine, but you're going to regret your decision one day, and then it will be too late."

I shoved a pair of jeans on and grabbed a shirt from the floor, pressing it down over me. "Fine, but I need to go." She turned on her heels, shaking her head and mumbling. I stepped into the bathroom and ran the toothbrush over my teeth. Wiping my face with a damp towel, I looked into the mirror. "She's right, I'm dumb, but I know deep down Bex deserves better," I told myself. Before I left, I searched the bed for the St Jude pendant, and found it tucked between the sheets. I dug it out, stuffed it into my pocket, and left.

***

When I opened the door to the vet clinic, the sounds of barking and yipping met me. "Good morning, Jackson," Milly greeted me.

I squinted and pressed my hands to my temples. "Not so loud."

"Haha, I heard about your escapades last night. In fact, we didn't expect to see you today."

"From who…? Never mind…Bex. So she's here."

"Yes, but she's not herself. Sadder even than after your letter."

"Geez, who all knows?"

"Son, this is a small town…everyone." She walked around and placed a hand on my shoulder. "Jackson, I had an uncle who lost his arm in the war. He felt the same as you do, though for him it was too late. After he let his girl go, she married someone else. By the time he realized his mistake, she'd died from a broken heart."

"I know, but Bex would be better off with another guy, one who could protect her. That's something I can't do anymore."

"Jackson, I feel it in my bones; you will regret letting that girl go."

I shook my head. "I doubt it."

She eyed me and quickly changed the subject. "Would you like to visit our new little guest?"

"Sure thing; where is he?"

"He's in the back."

I headed toward the kennels, but he wasn't in there. I saw Doc in his office. "Hey, Doc, where's the little puppy I brought in yesterday?"

"He's in recovery. He had to have emergency surgery last night."

"Why, what happened?"

His smile wavered. "You should go see him; I think he could use some visits."

Doc followed me to the back. Once in the recovery room, I looked in all the cages until I came to the one holding the puppy. "What happened? He was fine when I brought him back."

"Oh Jax, this is not your fault. He had an injury, probably from birth. Or maybe the people who had him hurt him. I did see evidence of a bullet wound...I'm just not one hundred percent certain. You know from experience; people are not always truthful when getting rid of animals."

I peered into the cage and the puppy was sound asleep. "Can I touch him?"

"Of course."

I reached in, and when my hand touched his soft fur I noticed his back end was bandaged. "Doc...no, you didn't!" He stared at me, his facial expression unreadable. "Did you have to remove his leg?"

He nodded. "But with your recent situation—"

"Why didn't you tell me?" I interrupted him.

He chuckled. "You really didn't give me the time to tell you. But yes, I had to remove the whole leg."

"Couldn't you have saved it?"

He looked over the puppy's chart and shook his head. "No, it was too far gone for saving."

"How come I didn't notice he was hurt when I picked him up?"

"We don't always see things that are so close to our own problems. Don't blame yourself; we didn't see it until we did a full workup." He patted me on the shoulder. "Maybe you can help him become accustomed to his injury. After all, he has a long road ahead of him. You know, if he doesn't learn to walk again he may not have the will to live." He winked at me.

I nodded. "What can I do?"

"You'll figure it out." He smiled at me and patted me on the back. "I'll leave you two alone.

I looked at the little guy all sprawled out. I wondered if it was the same for animals to lose a limb as it was for humans. Would he have phantom pains and so on? I ruffled his fur. "It'll be okay, little fella." He picked up his little head

67

and nosed my hand. "Are you hungry?" I glanced around and saw the IV bag connected to a tube in his front leg. He dropped his head back down and whined a bit. "It'll be okay, I promise."

I hoped it would. After about an hour of sitting with him in my lap and continually checking his vitals, I left the room with my thoughts heavy from the little dog's predicament.

CHAPTER

9

First thing the next morning I woke early and headed downstairs. "Hello, Mom."

"Hey, Jax. Where are you off to so early this morning?"

"Doc's to help out. There is a special puppy who needs some extra time with me."

She cocked her head at me. "Is that so, son?"

I laughed. "Yes, Mom." I grabbed a piece of toast and coffee and headed out the door. For the entire drive to the clinic my thoughts were plagued with the little puppy. I pulled into a parking spot and sighed when I saw Bex's car out front. "Well shit, this is not going to be a good day."

I opened the door and barking consumed the entire room. As I entered, I saw Milly sitting behind the desk and speaking to Bex. When they saw me, Bex stood and walked off.

"Don't mind her."

I nodded and smiled. "So, how's our little guest doing this morning?"

"Fine. He's up but not eating yet. Maybe you can get him to eat."

"I'll try."

"That's all we ask." She smiled at me over her glasses, then dropped her head to focus on the calendar of today's surgeries.

Hesitantly I stood and sauntered down the hallway. Through the window of the storage room I saw Bex standing with her back to me. Before I could stop myself I pushed the door open and entered. As I walked further inside she stared off out the window, I assumed watching the dogs.

"Bex."

She didn't move so I stepped inside. She turned around, tears brimming at the corners of her eyes. "What the hell do you want?" she said, wiping away the tears. "Why can't you just leave me alone? Stop showing up and pretending you still don't care."

I walked up closer to her. "I want you to understand why we can't be together."

She turned away from me and I gripped her shoulders. "I give up, Jax. Live your life alone forever. I really don't give a rat's ass what you do." She raised a hand and the crack against my cheek stung. My head swung backwards at the force of her slap. My soul burned like the desert sun, knowing deep down I was making a mistake pushing the woman I loved away. I just didn't know how to be the man I used to be.

I wanted desperately to comfort her, to feel her body pressed up against mine. But that was just old emotions coming back. I removed my hands from her shoulders. "I wish you the best, and never wanted to hurt you."

She turned, her face stoic. "Well, good lord, Jax. Save that sanctimonious shit for someone who cares."

I stepped back a bit and folded my arms over my chest. "You know, Bex, I don't need this shit."

"Good; then why don't you leave? I wish you'd never came back." Her anger consumed her soft features. I'd never seen her so angry.

"Damn it, Bex." The pit of my stomach churned as the words left my mouth.

"I was doing fine until you walked back into my life. You keep pushing me away and I don't know how to help you." She stormed past me, catching me off balance, and I had to grip onto a shelf to stop myself from toppling over. I passed a hand down my chin and sighed.

After a few minutes, when my heart was beating normally, I left the room and headed down to the recovery room. My heart ached with the weight of my decision to let Bex go. Part of me wondered if I was being giant idiot. But as I headed down the narrow hallway I knew other things deserved my attention; the Bex situation had to wait.

The room's atmosphere was alive with the beeping and buzzing of all the machines. I went over to the cage holding my little friend. When I peered inside, the puppy's back faced the door.

"Hello, little one." He didn't stir, so I opened the cage. He moved away from me. "Oh, come on, let's get you a bite to eat."

Carefully I scooped him into my arms, careful of all the tubes. With my other hand, I dragged the IV pole over to a table and placed him down. He shivered.

"Hold on, let me get you a heating pad." I grabbed a pad and a towel. Once they were on the table, I plugged the heating pad in and placed him on top. Quickly I began to empty a can of wet food, then sniffed it. "Yuck." I looked back over at the pup, who cocked his head at me slightly. "Sorry, I'm sure it tastes great." I dipped my finger and offered him some, but he turned his head away. "Come on, you gotta eat to keep your strength up."

"If he doesn't eat we will have to force feed him, and I don't want to have to do that." Doc walked in carrying a cat, and placed the feline in a kennel.

"I know; I'll try and get him to eat. Got any peanut butter?"

"Sure." He dug in the cabinet and brought me the jar.

"Thanks."

He nodded. "An old time go to bribery, huh Jax."

"Yep, I've never had it fail." I scooped out a spoonful and mixed it with the dog food, then coated my finger with the mixture and offered it to him. Again he turned his head. "Come on, pup." I stuck my finger under his nose. He sniffed and reached out his tongue. I held my breath, not moving a muscle so as not to scare him. With my finger still, I let him reach out and lick the food off. "That's it. Want some more?" He tried to stand up but toppled over. As he lay sprawled out on the table, he licked my finger again. After the third lick, he curled back into a ball on the table. I petted his head. "You did good today; we'll try a little more in a couple of hours."

"Good work, Jackson."

I smiled. "The peanut butter never fails."

He patted me on the shoulder. "No, it doesn't. But maybe you both need each other. Hey, Jackson, can you keep an eye on him tonight? I'm kinda short staffed, and you know what to do if something goes wrong."

"I don't know. Don't you have someone else, like Bex?"

He shook his head. "No, she has plans tonight."

Hesitantly I thought about it, not really wanting to, but then resigned myself to a night alone with no one bitching at me. "Sure thing. Let me grab a few essentials and a bite to eat from the house."

He nodded. "He'll be okay until you get back. Try to get a nap in...he'll need your full attention."

"Yes, sir." I took the puppy and placed him back in his kennel, where he curled up into a half ball with a bandage covering where his leg used to be. "Looks like we may have something in common, little guy." I petted his head and he licked my hand, then curled back up. "I'll be back, little guy."

A few hours later, after a nap, I returned to an empty clinic. Well, Milly and Bex had left, but Doc was still there.

"Hey, Jackson, you're back."

"Yeah, just had to get some provisions." I patted the duffle bag over my shoulder.

"Do you happen to have some bribery items in that bag?" He chuckled.

I laughed. "You know it. At least I'll get him to eat." I figured if I was stuck here, might as well make the most of it.

"Well good. I'll call you later to check on you both."

"Yes, sir; we'll be fine."

I watched as Doc left the room, then headed to the break room and tossed my duffle bag on the bed. Humming to myself, I pulled a frozen pizza out and shoved it in the microwave. I dropped down on the bed and thought, *What in the hell have I gotten myself into? It looks like another situation I can't seem to get out of...taking care of a hurt puppy, with the same hurt I am experiencing.*

The beeping of the microwave jerked me from the ramblings in my head. I stood and grabbed the pizza, then headed to the recovery room. A small whine emanated from the cage. A black nose stuck out between the metal wires of the cage and sniffed in my direction.

"Hey fella, you up?" I walked over to him, and his tail wagged slightly. "You hungry?"

He wagged his tail a little more, so I unlatched his kennel and lifted him up in my arms, making sure to grab the IV pole. "Well, come on then. Do you like pepperoni?" A little bark escaped his mouth. "Good, then I think I can share. Here you go." I offered him a slice of pepperoni and he gently picked at it, then licked it, finally gobbling it up.

I bit into a piece and let the cheese fall onto the table. The puppy sprawled out, trying to scoot on his belly over to the cheese. "You want this?" I laughed. He barked, so I pulled some cheese from another piece and dangled it in the air. "You have to come get it." He cocked his head from side to side, then scooted over to the ooey gooey cheese. He slurped it down in one fast movement. "Good boy."

After we were done, we both headed into the break room to rest. We sat down on the cot and I flipped the TV on with the remote. The puppy crawled up into my lap and I heard a little sigh. "What ya feel like watching?" He looked up at me with round eyes and barked. "Not sure yet, huh." I flipped the channels, trying to find something worth watching. "Nothing really, huh little dude."

He barked and wiggled around in my lap. "Oh, I bet you need to go outside. Let's go then." I scooped him up, pushed the IV pole ahead of us, and we headed out back to the fenced in yard. I placed him down on the grass. "Go on." He whined. I shook my head. "No, I can't help you with this." He wobbled a little, then he seemed to do his business. He yipped at me but I stared into the sky. The moon lit up the ground.

A sudden memory came crashing down of a time with Bex and me out at the park with a moon just like this. I'd asked her to the senior prom and she'd said yes. And afterwards we stayed at the cabin.

I dislodged the memory and looked down at the puppy. He sat wagging his tail back and forth. "You ready to go back inside?" He tried to stand but flopped over on his side. "You've got this."

He glanced up at me and barked, then stood and balanced himself. After a wobbly moment he slowly walked up to me. Then as he reached my boots he fell backwards.

"That's good for tonight." I laughed and picked him up, making sure to push the IV pole carefully. "Take it easy for tonight. I should know, after all." We headed back inside. "Hey, I think we have some more peanut butter. It'll help with your energy."

"Woof woof," he barked.

"Well then, let's get you some and see if anything is on TV now." After we were settled back in the staff room with the bowl of peanut butter, I flipped on the TV. As I flipped the channels I stopped on a movie, one I'd seen before. In fact, it was one of my favorites.

The pup sat on my lap and snuggled, licking peanut butter off his nose. He began to whine. "What's the matter?" He whined some more. "I bet you need another dose of pain medication." I rolled open the roller clasp and let the medicine drip down the tube. He settled back into my lap as I petted him. After a few moments he began to snore. Soon the sounds from the TV were a distant noise as I followed the puppy and fell asleep.

CHAPTER 10

I woke to find Bex staring at me angrily. No idea how long she'd been standing there, or tapping her foot for that matter, but there was no denying she was pissed. Before I rolled over I checked for the puppy.

"I put him back in his kennel," she said, glaring at me.

I sat up and wiped my face. "What's wrong, Bex?"

"Besides the obvious, Jax, I came in here and one of our patients, who had his leg amputated, was laying sprawled over you."

For the first time in months, my face etched into a grin. "Bex, I wouldn't have let anything happen to him."

"You sure? I mean, what if you had rolled over on him and hurt him."

I scoffed. "But I didn't."

"No, but you could've."

"Come on, Bex. What's the real issue here?"

She turned her back to me. "Can you just leave, Jax?" she said through sobs. "It's too hard for me to see you every day, knowing you no longer love me."

I stood and turned her by the shoulders to face me. "Bex, I do love you. It's just that you deserve better than me." She looked up at me, her eyes red from tears and her pouty lips begging for me to kiss them. Before I could stop myself, I pushed her up against the wall and leaned down. The moment my lips touched hers I knew I needed to stop, but I couldn't. For a brief second she returned the kiss, then pulled back as the tears slid down her face, and hauled off and slapped me. My head flung to the side, and when I regained my composure, she had walked out, slamming the door. Well, what the fuck had I done? I thought Bex was correct; I needed to leave her be.

I sighed, gathered my belongings, and stalked out of the break room. As I headed down the hallway I didn't run into Bex.

Milly sat behind her desk as I walked toward the door. "Morning, Jackson. How are you this morning? And better yet, how's our little patient?"

"He's doing good, ma'am," I mumbled.

I placed my hand on the knob and Milly stood behind me. "What's wrong, Jackson?"

"Nothing. I need to take a break from here and let Bex not have to see me every day."

Her hand rested on my forearm. "She just needs time. Maybe if you both have time you'll realize what a mistake you are making."

I turned to face her. "Honestly, I don't know what to think anymore."

She placed a hand on my chest. "You need to follow your heart." At her touch, an electrical pulse penetrated my heartbeat.

"Whoa, what was that?"

"Nothing...just helping you to open your heart again. Now go home and think, and when you come back, hopefully you will see more clearly."

I nodded. "It may be awhile. Please take care of the puppy, and make sure he gets the best care."

"Oh, I certainly will. You sure you don't want to...? Never mind...maybe when you come back. Jackson, take all the time you need, but don't be gone too long. I think our little friend needs you."

I turned back and opened the door. "I won't, but I do think Bex needs some time."

CHAPTER 11

Two weeks later

I opened the door to the clinic and looked around. Milly looked up from the desk and smiled. "You're back."

"Yes, ma'am." The low yipping of a puppy alerted me. From around the desk, a little black head popped out. "Hello, little guy." I walked over and knelt down. "Come here, little man." The puppy didn't move at all, just peeked around the corner. His ears were floppy and he had grown some. "What's wrong with him?"

"I think he's missed you." She looked down at him and urged him to me. "Go ahead." He glanced from her to me then padded over and nuzzled my hand.

Changing the subject, I said, "Milly, he looks like a rotty."

"Yes, except he's short and long like a basset hound."

"Hey, fella. So what's your name?"

Milly spoke up. "I've been calling him Bullet."

I scooped up the dog and his one back leg dangled. "Well, that's a great name." I gripped the necklace around my neck with the bullet on it as a remembrance of what I'd been through. Suddenly a flashback hit me.

As I lay in the dirt waiting for the medics to come and get me, the pain in my body burned through my veins, bones, and skin. I blacked out as sturdy hands lifted me up, placing me on a gurney. "Watch the leg," I heard a voice say.

"Damn it to hell, it's hanging on by a thread," someone else said.

Oh no, *I thought, then darkness invaded me.*

I shook my head, dislodging all the painful memories. I glanced up at Milly, realizing I was on the floor.

"Are you all right?"

"Yes," I nodded as the puppy crawled into my lap.

"I think he likes you, Jackson."

"At least someone doesn't judge me for my decisions, huh little guy." I ruffled his fur. He curled up into my lap and yawned.

"Why don't you foster him for a while?"

"Eh, I don't know."

"Are you worried about Debra?"

I laughed, knowing everyone knew of my mother's OCD about not having a dog in the house. "A little."

"We could really use the help. We got an influx of dogs who are sick, and I would hate for him to be exposed much longer. Besides, I think you could help him in his transition to walking on three legs. He hasn't been walking much since you've been gone." She smiled. "I'm sure once your mother sees him she'll fall for him as well."

"I don't know about that."

The puppy looked up and barked at me. Chuckling, I scratched him behind his ears. "I guess it wouldn't hurt. Besides, he's sure to find a home soon. Wanna go home with me, Bullet?"

He barked loudly as Bex walked in. "What are you doing here?" Anger in her voice masked the sadness.

"Becki, he's fostering Bullet."

"Oh, whatever." She stalked away, her head low.

I shook my head as her figure retreated down the hall.

"Jackson, you should talk to her."

"I don't think she wants to talk to me."

"Well, you should try."

"I don't know." I looked down at the puppy. "What do you think, Bullet?"

Round eyes stared up at me, then he opened his mouth and yipped.

"Then I guess it's settled. I'll go talk to her. Here, you stay with Milly. We don't want you to get sick."

I walked into the back and passed Bex in the hallway on the way. "Hi, Bex."

She turned to face me. "No Jax, you don't get to pretend like everything is a-okay." She made the sign of quotation marks with her fingers.

"Bex, don't be like that."

She looked at me, anger and hatred coursing through her expression. "Don't be like what, Jax?" She hit me in the chest with her finger.

"Mad!" I backed up. I'd never seen her like this before, and I was the cause.

"Oh shit, Jax...don't be a jackass," she scoffed.

"I'm not being a—"

"Yes, you are. You are giving up on life, and I don't want to be a part of your stupidity."

"Good. I hope you are finally moving on." As the words tumbled out of my mouth I regretted them instantly.

"No. But you keep pushing me away and I can't keep fighting you. And if you insist on working here, just stay the hell away from me," she spat.

"Fine, Bex." I turned on my heels and stormed back up front.

****

Milly sat cooing at the puppy that kept licking her face. She looked up when I walked out. "Didn't go very well, did it?"

I shook my head. "I didn't really think it would."

"No, but do you blame her, Jax? She's hurting, so she has to punch back."

I sat in a chair across from her, watching the puppy. "No. The sooner she realizes I'm not the one for her, the sooner she can move on. I never imagined when I came here she would be working here too."

She put the puppy down on the floor and he padded around to me unsteadily. He stopped at my feet, begging me to pick him up. I scooped him up and placed him on my lap. Scratching his ears, I let the movement comfort me.

"Looks like he has become fond of you."

"I guess," I said, melancholy.

"Look, Jax, I think I may be able to help you."

"With what?"

"Your little dilemma of not feeling a hundred percent man."

I chuckled loudly. "The only way that could change is if my leg grew back, and we know that will never happen."

She shook her head. "Maybe you aren't ready yet."

I shrugged my shoulders and stood, cradling the puppy to my chest. "I think we'd better get going before Bex comes back."

"Have a nice day, Jax." She stood and handed me a bag. "I'll call you when you can bring him back. He's also had his first and second set of shots."

"What's this?"

"A few supplies for the little guy. And some bandage changes. We don't want him getting infected. I'm sure you know how to change a bandage?"

"Thanks. I do."

I grabbed the bag and walked out to my truck. Opening the door was a challenge since I had a sleeping puppy in my arms along with the bag of supplies, so I dropped the bag carefully on the ground and unlocked the door. Afterward I gently placed Bullet on the seat, nudging him over a bit. Then I picked up the bag and placed it on the floorboard of the passenger side. After I slid in, I started the vehicle. Pulling out of my parking spot, I drove the car down the street, heading home with my new companion on my lap.

CHAPTER

12

When we pulled into the driveway Bullet woke and began to squirm on my lap. He barked and barked. "What's wrong fella?"

He yipped again.

I hurriedly put the car into park and opened the door. He almost leapt from my lap, but I caught him before he landed on the ground. "Watch out. You gotta be careful, little dude."

I placed him on the ground and he hobbled around, sniffing every blade of grass, every bug that hopped past him. He bent down low in the grass like a cat and put his butt in the air, wiggling it every second or so. In front of him sat a butterfly. It flapped its wings furiously, but Bullet just stared back at it. I leaned against the truck, crossed my arms behind my head, and watched him.

My father walked up to me. "What do we have here, son?"

"An orphan pup from Doc's."

"What happened to him?"

"His leg was damaged, so they had to remove it."

He eyed me with concern. "Hmmm. I'm sure your mother won't mind, as long as it's not for long."

I shook my head and knelt down as Bullet toddled over to me. "I'm sure you will find a home soon, won't you?"

"Woof," he responded as he jumped up, placing his stubby front paws on my knee while balancing on the one back leg.

"Yeah, I'm sure he will." He patted me on the shoulder. "I'll go warn your mother that we have a houseguest."

"We'll be in as soon as he finishes out here." I pushed Bullet back into the grass. "Go on. You won't win any sympathy if you use the bathroom in the house." After I let him play a few more minutes I called him to me. "All right, Bullet, come." He turned his head and sat, wagging his tail. "Come on boy." I patted my knee. He trotted towards me, running into my shoe. He fell backward, but soon righted himself.

"Still haven't gotten the hang of it, huh. It takes time." I caressed the puppy on his head and stood. "Come on, let's meet the family."

"Yip, yip."

He bounded off ahead of me, skidding and rolling head over butt to a stop at the door. I opened the door and he ran full steam ahead, as if a tornado had blown him into the house. I laughed. It seemed he was learning rather quickly how to get around with three legs. He bounded through room after room like a whirling dervish.

"What the hell?" I heard my mother exclaim as I heard crashes coming from the kitchen. "Jackson Hamilton Ledet!" she screamed. "What is this little terror running through my house?"

I got to the kitchen in time to see Bullet on the floor chewing on tonight's dinner. He tugged, trying to drag the piece of meat on the floor, as my mother sat on the ground with her legs sprawled out around her, the pot roast on the floor a few feet away from her.

"Mom, I see you've met our new houseguest," I chuckled, and leaned against the fridge.

"Is that so, son?"

"Yes, Mom."

I laughed even harder as Bullet climbed on my mom to lick the gravy from the roast that had splattered from landing on the floor. I saw a hint of a grin on her face, but it quickly disappeared when she saw me smiling.

"Well, get him off me," she chastised me. "Now I've got to come up with something else to eat tonight, since this little hellion ruined dinner."

I scooped him up and held him in my arms as he tried to wiggle out of them. "Not a good first impression," I whispered to him.

"What's all the racket in here?" My dad entered and burst out laughing at my mom still sprawled on the floor.

"Hey Dad, it looks as if Bullet and Mom met."

He walked over to her and helped her up. "It seems so."

She eyed him. "This is not funny, John."

He laughed. "Oh, but it is, Debra."

She slapped him on the shoulder. "Well, Mr. Funny Guy, what do you think we will do since the little rat ate your dinner?"

They both looked over at us and my father laughed. "It must have been good."

I looked down at Bullet and he was licking his chops, trying to reach a smidge of gravy he couldn't quite reach on the bridge of his nose.

"Mom and Dad, why don't you go out to eat, on me?" I reached into my pocket and handed a few bills to her.

"Oh, all right. But one question; how long is he staying?" she asked with her nose turned up at the puppy.

"Not long. I'm sure he'll find a home soon."

"Debra, Jax is helping Doc out with an orphaned puppy." My father took my mother's arm, removed the apron and placed it over a chair, then dragged her away.

"But you know how I feel about dogs in the house."

"Don't be hard on the animal; besides, don't you think it would be good for Jax to have a friend?"

"I guess. But couldn't he—?"

"Shhh. Let's go eat."

After my parents left, I shook my head and looked down at Bullet. "Not a very good first impression at all, little buddy. You will be working this off for a long time." His only reply was to reach up and lick my face. "Let's get you situated while you stay here."

I placed him back on the floor. He made a beeline for the roast, and I quickly picked it up before he reached the hunk of meat. I wrapped it in some foil from the counter and tossed it in the garbage can. He put his paws on my leg, curious about what I was doing. After I replaced the lid on the garbage can, I looked down at him. "Now don't you go near that garbage can. You must learn not to upset my mother."

"Woof woof," he barked in agreement.

I grabbed the bag of supplies from where I'd left them on the chair before all the chaos had happened. I emptied the food and bowl, leaving them in the kitchen. "Why don't we go watch a movie?" He barked and ran around my feet, wagging his tail.

Before heading into the family room, I grabbed a beer and some chips. I picked a movie and let the DVD slide into the player. After I'd sat down, I patted the sofa beside me, letting him know it was okay to jump up. He struggled to climb up on the cushion. He kicked his one stubby back leg, but it did not offer much help.

"Here, let me get you." I lifted him up. "Now don't go ratting me out to Mom."

"Woof."

"Good boy." I patted him on the head and offered him a chip, which he snatched out of my hand. "You still hungry?" He looked up at me, his eyes wide, begging for another salty chip as drool hung from his open mouth. "I don't know if these are good for you. Besides, you ate half a roast." He looked at me then at the bag of chips, then prowled over and pounced on the bag, dragging it over to the other side of the sofa. "Oh no you don't, you little rascal." I grabbed the chips and held them out of his reach. He whined a little, then curled up and snuggled beside me, probably hoping I'd drop a crumb or two.

CHAPTER 13

The next morning, still on the sofa, I woke to a weight on my chest. I squinted one eye open to see two wide brown eyes staring at me, then before I could stop it a pink tongue darted out. He wagged his tail and his whole body wiggled with the movement.

"Look who's up," I heard my sister say from the chair opposite me.

I rolled over carefully, letting the puppy slide to the floor. He rolled and kicked his feet in the air, then quickly righted himself. "Good morning to you, Suzie."

Bullet padded over to her, begging to be picked up.

"So, brother, where did you get this little fellow?" she asked as she lifted him up.

I pushed myself to a sitting position and stretched. "From Doc's, and no, he's not staying here forever. He'll get a home. We are just fostering him."

My sister tilted her head at me and grinned. "Yeah sure, that's what you say now." She eyed his back leg. "What happened to him?"

I shrugged. "Not sure. I rescued him from some people that probably hurt him. There were animal traps all over the place when I picked him up. Maybe he got caught in one, but Doc said he could have been shot."

"Oh no!"

"It's okay; he'll be all right."

"Like you, brother?" She cocked an eyebrow at me. She laughed as Bullet placed his paws on her chest and licked her face. "See, this little guy knows the truth."

He barked in agreement then jumped off her lap, landing on his belly with all three legs spread out. I shook my head. "Dust it off, little fella; you're fine." He looked up at me and yipped.

"You should follow your own advice and stop being so damn stubborn."

"Damn it, you too? For shit's sake, does anyone not know I wrote a letter to Bex?"

She grinned over at me. "The perks of living in a small town, dear brother." She winked at me and stood up. "Well, I need to head out; I've got studying to get done."

I nodded. "See ya later, Suzie."

I sat up, picked up my prosthesis from the floor, and hooked it to my stump. After I had it in place I stood and ambled into the kitchen. The dog food sat on the counter, so I poured some into the small metal bowl, the kibble making the only sound in the eerily quiet kitchen. "Okay, hurry up, Bullet." He skidded to his bowl and gobbled up the kibble. "So what do you want to do today?" Bullet didn't respond, just kept scarfing down his food. I turned on the coffee maker and headed upstairs to dress while he ate breakfast.

Once I'd finished I made my way downstairs. Bullet sat by the bottom of the steps with his leash in his mouth. "Where did you find that, boy?"

My answer came quickly as I heard my mother holler, "Dammit, Jackson Hamilton Ledet."

I eyed the puppy. "Now you've gone and done it. She never curses along with my full name unless she's really mad."

Bullet ran off towards the kitchen, the leash trailing and whipping around behind him. I followed, shaking my head. The moment I stepped one foot in the kitchen I burst out laughing. There was the paper bag Milly had given me in pieces, strewn from one end of the kitchen to the other; dog food littered the hardwood floor.

My mother stood tapping her foot with her hands on her hips. "Jackson, this little hellion is going to give me a heart attack."

I glanced behind me and Bullet sat on his haunches with his head hung. "Oh, come on Mom...look at him. He's sorry." His head popped up when he heard me talking about him. He walked over to my mother and whined.

She looked down at him and softened her expression. "There will be some rules put into place if you plan on staying here."

I laughed out loud. "Mom, this is only temporary."

She gave me the mom look with raised brows, then picked up Bullet. "Don't you listen to him, but you must learn a few rules of the house."

I shook my head as she walked off. My whole damn family consisted of a bunch of softies.

I drank my coffee at the kitchen table and waited for their return from a tour of the house and learning the house rules. Bullet skidded in and stopped abruptly at the edge of my chair. He looked up at me and barked.

"I guess you are ready to go?" He sat and wagged his tail. "And that would be a yes, I assume." I stood and he darted out in front of me, careening down the hallway on three legs.

Guess he was learning how to handle himself. He stopped suddenly, bouncing off the door. "Careful, little guy."

"Of course, Jackson. Puppies, like babies, can overcome hurdles. You should take a play from his playbook."

I laughed. "Yes, Mom."

"You really should think about keeping him. I think he will do you some good."

"But Mom, you called him a rat and a hellion."

"Yes, but that was before we had an agreement."

I chuckled. "So, now you are a dog whisperer?"

She stared at me with sadness and a bit of hope. "Son, ever since you brought him into my house you've been happy and acted like the young man I raised." She stopped and looked over at Bullet sitting by the door with his leash dangling from his mouth. "I don't know how he did it, but he seems to make you need him and he needs you. Go with it, son, and maybe—just maybe—your soul will heal." She wiped at her eyes, turned, and walked into the kitchen.

CHAPTER

14

The hot southern sun beat down on Bullet and me as we headed to my truck. I glanced down to see him running after a bug, his nose to the ground and his ass up in the air, his tail going a mile a minute. I leaned against my truck, crossing one booted foot over the other, and waited. He darted across the yard back and forth, stopping every time he heard a sound. His ears would perk up, then he would drop them and continue off after a bug or a lizard.

My dad walked up and puffed on his cigar.

"Hey, Dad, what's up?"

He took a long draw and blew out smoke. "Not much, son."

I cracked a grin at him. "So Dad, when did you start smoking cigars? You know those things will kill you."

His eyebrows shot up and he hurriedly looked around. "A few of the guys do when we are out on the boat. It takes the boredom out of not catching any fish."

"Uh huh. Don't let Mother catch you, or you'll be in more trouble than our three-legged friend here." I pointed in the direction of the puppy. He was scooting along the grass on his belly after a green lizard. I watched his almost soldier-like movements as he slid after the reptile.

My father elbowed me. "Resemble anyone you know?" he asked, holding the cigar from his mouth. I turned back to watch the stealthy movements of the black and tan dog. "You know, he seems to be acclimated to the life he now lives." He eyed me with a questioning look.

"I know...much better than me, huh Dad."

"Give it time. Though believe it or not, I think that dog is making you realize what life has to offer you and him."

I nodded and smiled at the puppy running and tumbling in the grass. "Dad, for once I'll admit I think you're right."

He glanced from me to Bullet. "Well, it's about damn time you admitted that," he laughed.

I grinned back at him. "If you tell anyone, including Mom, I'll deny it all and say you are getting senile."

"Ha, your mother already thinks that anyway, so that argument won't fly with her."

"Yeah, you're right." I looked down at Bullet, who sat in front of me wagging his tail, making swishing sounds on the grass.

"How's Bex?"

"Dad, not now."

"Have you given any thought to changing your mind about her?"

Changing the subject, I said, "Hey Dad, you feel like taking the boat out and showing our new friend the joys of fishing?"

He slapped my back. "Don't you need to see Doc?"

"No, Bullet and I are quarantined for a bit since he's only had a few shots."

He nodded. "Well then, son, I would love a day out on the water with you and this little fella. Go get the boat ready and I'll tell your mom. Maybe she can pack us a lunch."

"Okay Dad." I glanced down to see Bullet back in the grass chasing another bug. "Bullet!" He popped his head up. "Come on boy, let's go get the boat ready." He turned and ran towards me, and we both made our way to the boat shed.

After Bullet and I had made sure that the boat was ready with poles and bait, we waited for Dad to join us.

"Hey, son, you ready?" He walked up with enough food for an army.

"Geez, does Mom plan on us being away forever?"

"You know how she is; she wants us prepared for the inevitable."

"Yeah, like us not catching any fish," I laughed.

When my dad stepped into the boat, he placed the basket down and Bullet went straight over to it.

"No Bullet."

He stopped mid sniff and looked up at me, his round eyes begging me to let him have one morsel.

"Jackson, your mom packed something for him too," Dad said from his position at the bow of the boat.

I reached down and petted Bullet, then dug around in the basket. As I pulled out a cookie, Bullet jumped around on three legs. "Here boy. Now, there's more, but we need to ration our food because Mom seems to think we'll be lost out on the lake."

The boat puttered to life and Dad headed to our favorite fishing spot. Bullet stood up at the stern balancing on his back leg, his little tail wagging like a boat propeller as Dad steered the boat.

Dad coaxed the boat to a stop and turned to me. "You ready?"

I nodded, dug out the worms, and wiggled one in front of Bullet, who snapped at it as it curled away from him. Sticking the wiggling worm to a hook, I tossed my line into the water and waited. Bullet placed both front paws on the side of the boat and looked over to where I'd tossed the line. He looked back to me, then back to the murky water. I propped my foot up on the side and leaned back, waiting for a fish to take the bait. "Bullet, keep an eye on my line for me."

He wiggled his butt and barked low. My dad sat on the opposite side of me, which signaled our long time competition of who caught the most fish; we had points for types of fish and quantity. As I leaned back my line tugged a bit, and when I glanced over at Bullet, his attention was focused on the little orange bob in the water. Another tug and another one, then the line plunked into the water. "Woof."

I sat up and waited for the bob to go under the water a bit more. Once my line went tight, I started winding my reel, slowly pulling the line. The fish tugged and pulled, but I kept a steady hand and let the fish get tired. Slowly I reeled in my fish that had no intention of being caught. The more the fish fought, the more Bullet wagged his tail.

Finally, after a tough fight, I pulled and flung the fish onto the boat. Bullet snapped at the fish as it flew and landed on the bottom by the ice chest. "Leave it, Bullet; we need to clean it and cook it. We don't eat sushi in this family, but we do fry it up."

The rest of the day Dad and I fished and Bullet kept an eye out. At one time, after I'd caught more than my Dad, Bullet switched sides and decided to help him...I could only assume...to beat me. After quite a catch, we headed back home to clean the fish and have a fish fry.

Mother was waiting for us when we arrived home. Bullet placed his paws on the edge of the boat and waited for us to dock. When we did, I helped him out and placed him on the wooden walkway. He sat on his haunches, watching me grab the fish and hoist them out. One flopped out of the ice chest and fell to the ground.

"Don't you dare."

He eyed me, then scooped up the fish and ran off with the head and tail dangling from the sides of his mouth.

"Oh, Jackson, let him have one; after all, he did help us catch them."

I laughed and picked up the ice chest. "You're right. Let's get these cleaned and prepped for dinner." I followed Bullet and watched him zig zag away from my sister, who tried to get the fish from him. "Suzie, let him have it."

"No!" she hollered. "It has to be cooked."

In an instant he dropped it and she picked it up. I headed to the back yard, happy for the first time in a very long time. I missed Bex, but that could no longer be helped.

After all the fish had been fried to a crisp, I snapped a small piece off and tossed it to Bullet. "Now this is how you eat fish." He gobbled it and begged for more.

"Wait, we have to wait for our guests." Mom came out carrying a huge bowl of potato salad.

"What guests—?"

"Debra, let me get that for you." My father interrupted me, taking the bowl and placing it on the table.

"Wait, what guests?" I questioned again. Before anyone answered me, Ben and Bex came walking into the yard. "Mom, what did you do?"

She smiled and gritted her teeth. "You will be nice to her...I had to beg her to come. Now go offer to help her carry the dessert."

"Damn it, Mom," I muttered, wishing she'd stay out of this.

"Debra dear, you need to stay out of this," I heard my dad tell her.

"No. I'm tired of him being stupid."

He shook his head as I walked, trying to plaster on a smile for Bex.

My sister pushed past me as another car pulled into the drive. "Don't be an ass in front of my boyfriend."

"What boyfriend?" I asked as I took the cake from Bex and smiled. "Hi, Bex and Ben." I whispered to Bex., "Sorry for my mother's meddling."

"It's okay. You know I love your mother." She walked away, leaving me with Ben.

"Jax, you really are being stupid; that woman loves you."

"Not you too."

He grinned. "Sorry, I tell it like it is. And you, my friend, are a huge dumbass."

"Look, let's just agree to disagree."

"Whatever, man, but you are still a dumbass." He laughed, walking backwards to taunt me.

"Watch out, Ben!"

But he never heard me as he tumbled backwards into the grass. Bullet ran over, jumping on him and licking him in the face.

I bent down, balancing the dessert, and laughed. "Look who's the dumbass now."

"Come on, both of you; let's eat," my mother said. My sister came over to the table holding the hand of some guy.

"Dan, I would like you to meet my brother." Her eyes lit up when she said his name.

I remembered that look...it was the same one Bex use to wear. I looked over to her and her head was down. I wished Mother hadn't brought her here. This was so hard on her. For an instant I thought to go over and comfort her, but that would only lead her on. The sooner she moved on and the sooner my mother realized it, the better everyone would be.

"Nice to meet you." The young man offered his hand.

"Same here," I nodded.

"Jax, come sit here next to Bex."

I hesitated, but then did as she requested. When I sat down I mouthed, "Sorry." She bit her lip to keep from crying. My heart went out to her; I would have to ask my mom to let this go.

After dinner Suzie and her boyfriend left to see a movie at the cinema. I looked around for Bex, but she wasn't anywhere around.

"She had Ben take her home." My mom walked in, carrying dishes from outside.

"She did?"

"Yes." Her face was sad, but she never said another word.

I figured this was the end of her trying to get us back together.

CHAPTER 15

Three weeks later

When I woke, Bullet lay beside me, his head on my pillow. I shook my head and rolled over in bed, careful not to disturb the dog. I padded downstairs and met my mother in the kitchen.

"Morning, Jackson. Milly called and said you and Bullet could come back today."

"Oh, good." I started to ask a question but stopped.

"She didn't say anything about Bex," my mother said as she cracked two eggs and began making an omelet.

"That's not what I was thinking."

She eyed me and smiled. "Sure it wasn't, son. Now sit and eat before you leave." A loud crash startled us. My mother stopped and peeked around the door frame. She screamed as Bullet came stampeding down the hall and around the corner. She held a hand over her heart. "Damn, that dog is going to give me a heart attack." He stopped suddenly and looked apologetic.

"Mom, he's sorry."

She shook her head. "I know son, I know," she said as she placed a bowl of food down for him. I burst out laughing when more of the food landed on the floor than in his mouth.

"Hurry up, Bullet. We get to go see Miss Milly today."

"Woof woof," he barked, then pushed the bowl around. I laughed out loud at the sight of my mother's squinched up face as the metal bowl scraped around on her hard wood floor. After we finished, we headed to the truck.

I opened the door to the clinic and Bullet made a beeline for Milly.

"Hello, little guy," she cooed at him.

"Hey, Miss Milly; is Bex here?"

"No, she's not. She decided to take some time off."

I dropped my head. "I don't blame her, especially with me here. Do you think I should find another place to volunteer?"

She looked over at me, and sadness crept into her expression. "Jackson, honestly, you need to stop being so damn stubborn. That girl loves you, no matter what."

"No, I'm no good for her."

She sat across from me. "Why do you feel that way?"

"Because I'm half a man now."

"Stop that shit. I think you need to speak to someone that can help you heal your soul."

I looked over at the dog, knowing Bullet was doing that very thing. I just couldn't help wanting more for Bex. "I'm not talking to a shrink."

She laughed loudly. "I'm not talking about a shrink. I'm talking about Ogun, loa of war."

"Wait a minute; are you talking about voodoo?"

"Yes," she smiled.

"Isn't that messing with dark forces?"

She laughed haughtily. "No, Jackson, you have been watching too much television. It is very similar to Catholicism."

"Hmmm, I don't know." A wave of hesitation passed over me.

"He is someone who may know what you are going through and can help you heal your thoughts...," she looked over at Bullet, "because it looks as if someone is helping you as well.

That little puppy knows what we all see inside; it might be time for you to hear it from another warrior. So that you may open your heart to Bex once again." She nodded towards Bullet, who was sound asleep at my feet.

"I'm not sure about this. Give me some time to think on it."

"Sure, no problem."

"I'll head into the back and walk the dogs."

She nodded, dropped her head, and scooped Bullet into her lap. I shuffled into the back, not really believing in this voodoo hoodoo shit. I'd already asked for help from every religious being known to man. I didn't think some warrior could help...or could he? I shook my head. "No, he can't."

I continued down the hallway to the dogs. On my way, I poked my head into Doc's office. "How ya doing, Doc?"

"Good, good, Jackson; how are you?"

"So so, sir."

"What's troubling you besides the obvious?"

I sighed and stood in the doorway of his office. "That's about it, Doc."

"Wanna talk about it?"

"Not really."

He smiled. "Well, you know if you ever want to I'm here for you."

"Yes, sir. Thanks. I'll get to work so Bullet and I can head home."

He smiled. "How's that going? How's Debra taking to having a dog in her house?"

I laughed out loud. "Well, Doc she wasn't happy at first after the roast beef fiasco, but apparently she and Bullet discussed the house rules." I leaned forward and whispered, "I think she is beginning to like him."

"Are you surprised? I think she realizes how much good he does for you, and vice versa. Speaking of, how's he getting along after the surgery? Have you thought about adopting him?"

Before I could answer, Bullet skidded into the room, bouncing off the wall as he tried to stop himself. "Well, it looks like he's acclimating to his injuries."

Doc laughed as he looked over his glasses at the puppy licking his paw and acting like his careening movements were done on purpose. "I see that."

"Well, I best get to work, Doc." I turned to Bullet. "Why don't you go play with Miss Milly?"

He barked and ran out of the room in the direction of the front office.

After I had walked every dog and cleaned every dog and cat's kennel, I headed out. Bullet was waiting for me when I came out of the back. He ran towards me, halting right before he ended up on my boot. "Ready to go home, fella?"

"I think he's been ready; he's been pacing by the door for the last hour."

I pick him up in my arms. "Well, I don't want to disappoint you; let's go, little buddy."

"Before you leave I have something for you, just in case you change your mind about what we discussed. Ogun will show you what you need to see, I promise you." She lifted a bag from the ground and handed it to me. "Here, take this and head off to the most wooded area you can find."

"What's in the bag?"

"Everything you need in order to speak to Ogun. But first, head on over to a crossroads and speak to Papa Legba."

"Are you kidding me?"

"No Jackson, I never kid about matters such as this. But if you wish to live your life in the present situation, then by all means, do not do as I ask you."

"What could it hurt?"

"That's right son, nothing. He may just be able to show you your worth."

I grabbed the bag.

"If you decide to do it, please leave Bullet at home."

"Why?"

She grinned and her face took on an unfamiliar expression. "Ogun likes meat. He may feel Bullet is part of his offering. That reminds me, if you don't want to kill an animal, he will take snails you've let go into the afterworld."

"Oh, okay. I still need time to think on this. I mean, I don't actually believe in voodoo."

"You will be fine. I wrote down instructions in the bag."

"Yes, ma'am." I shuddered at the thought of Milly practicing voodoo.

She nodded. "Be on your way."

I turned and left with Bullet in tow.

CHAPTER 16

As we walked out into the cool air, I sucked back a deep breath. "Okay," I mumbled under my breath. "What in the hell have I gotten into?"

"Woof!"

"Exactly my thoughts, little dude." We entered the truck and drove in silence all the way home. When we pulled into the drive, my parents' car sat in the driveway. "All right, behave yourself in front of Debra."

"Woof."

I opened the door and he flew out of the car, landing with a thud on the grass. He fell head over ass and landed on his back. He struggled to flip back over; not an easy feat with his stubby body. I chuckled. "You okay, little buddy?" I righted him and he whined. "Are you hurt?" He nuzzled up to me. "You little rascal; now do your business so we can get inside."

He ran around the yard at full speed, finally stopping. After he was finished, he ran back over to me, halting right in front of me.

"So how is the little thing doing?" My father met me outside with a beer in hand. "Want one?"

"Sure, thanks. He's doing fine."

"Any luck on finding him a home?" He eyed me over his beer.

"No, though Doc asked me if I had thought about adopting him."

"Oh, did he now?" A sly smile crossed his face.

I ignored it and changed the subject. "Work was really weird today."

"What happened?"

I thought it best not to tell my dad about Milly and her voodoo hoodoo shit. "Oh, nothing really."

He cocked his head at me and I assumed decided not to delve into any questions. But that thought was quickly squashed. "Did you see Bex today?"

"No, and I probably made her quit her job."

"Why? What do you mean?"

"Well, she took some time off."

"Oh well, is that all. She'll be back...she just needs some time."

"I guess...though I never meant to hurt her. I want what's best for her. I just wish Mom would have let it go and not invited her the other night."

"Your mother meant well." He leaned against my truck and looked up at the night sky. "Did you ever think you are what's best for her?"

"Please Dad, you know I'm no longer—"

"Jackson, did I ever tell you how I met your mother?"

"Yes."

I stared back up at the sky and watched as the stars twinkled. Memories of Bex flooded my thoughts, but they were interrupted by my dad. Before I could stop him, he continued his story as if I hadn't heard it before.

"Well anyway, it was much like this night." He continued to gaze up at the sky. "Do you know the old Harper land out on I-90, the one that had the old drive-in movies?"

I nodded, pretty much knowing this story by heart since they reminisced every anniversary.

"Well anyway, the moment I saw your mom at the snack bar I knew I wanted to know her more." He turned his head to face me. "She was an angel as she stood there holding a box of popcorn. But as you know, she had a boyfriend who beat her. Once she had him locked up, it took me many dates to convince her she and I belonged together." He turned back to look up to the sky, and without looking back at me he said, "Stop being stupid, son. Don't let Bex go; you only find that kind of love once. She doesn't care that you are injured. In fact, she has been concerned for you through the whole ordeal. She's orchestrated many a prayer list at church."

Bullet's barks interrupted our conversation. "You ready to go inside?"

He ran around in circles and the three of us walked up to the house. When the door opened, the smell of dinner permeated the house. My mother looked around the doorframe of the kitchen.

"Debra, that sure smells good." Dad walked off towards the kitchen.

"Come on, Bullet, let's get a bite to eat." The dog crept ahead of me.

"Hello, son and little rat," my mother greeted us.

"Debra, your jealousy is showing," my father laughed.

"John, just sit and eat. Jax, the dog will not be fed from the table. He knows the rules...I've already informed him."

I chuckled. "Yes, Mother. Let me get him fed then."

"Already done. I have set him up with his own place to eat."

"Mom!" I exclaimed, glancing at her, and she laughed.

"What do you take me for? I set him over by the door, not outside." She placed a bowl filled with food down on the floor. Bullet gobbled it up, but as soon as she turned and walked over to the table, he followed her.

"Shh," I said to him as he crawled under the table.

My mother rolled her eyes as she witnessed his retreating black tail. I sat still and Bullet whined from under the table. "Don't you dare feed him from the table."

I grinned and dug my fork into the scrumptious dinner that sat before me. "This is good, Mother." Bullet came from under the table and stood with his paws on my hip. "No, get down," I chastised him.

My sister ran into the house. "I'm sorry I'm late." She skidded to a stop at the table and sat down.

"No worries; you're here now. Eat."

My sister smirked at me. "So what's up, bro?"

"Not much, little sis." I scooped up some more food and bit into it, anger consuming me for some unknown reason.

From under the table, Bullet tried climbing up my prosthesis. "No, Bullet!" I shoved him off a little too hard and he slid across the floor, where he huddled in the corner and whined.

"Damn, Jax, you didn't need to hurt him."

"Language, Suzie."

"Jackson, what the hell is your problem?" Suzie glared at me. "Mother, I refuse to sit at the table with Mr. Pity Party table of one." My sister stood, knocking her drink over onto the table. My mother stood and grabbed a towel from the counter, and wiped up the liquid that had begun to drip onto the floor.

"Suzie, please," she pleaded with my sister.

"No." She went over to the puppy and scooped him up in her arms. "It's okay, little man. My brother's in a sour mood all of a sudden."

I glowered at her, not really coming to terms with what had made me mad. In fact, I really had no idea what had caused my anger. "Look, I didn't want him messing up my fake leg."

"Good god, Jax, like this little puppy could hurt that." Bullet snuggled in her arms, giving me the sad puppy dog look. "Mother, I am done eating," Suzie said, walking off with the puppy.

My mother shook her head and gave me a look. "What?"

"Nothing, Jackson." She bowed her head into her hands and softly cried.

I stood, causing my chair to fall to the floor. "I'm going to bed, since all of a sudden I'm the bad guy."

"It's okay, Debra, he just had a little setback. He's making progress...that puppy will continue to help him," my father said as I stomped off upstairs.

I left out a huff, and once in my bedroom I sat on the bed with my head in my hands. "How in the hell has my life turned out this way? I had such a promising life, and now I have nothing." I leaned back, closing my eyes tight and wishing the world would disappear and take me with it. I tossed and turned, trying hard to doze off. After about an hour, I slipped into sleep.

A voice pulled me from my slumber. "Jackson." I tossed on the mattress, wishing for the voice to be quiet. I rolled over and shoved the pillow over my head, but the voice didn't stop. "Jackson, come speak to me...I can help you. Bring me an offering."

I popped my eyes open wide at the eerie voice calling to me. Before I could change my mind, I grabbed the bag Milly had given me and headed outside. I stopped to open the bag and pulled out Milly's note.

Go to two streets that cross each other, leave the offerings in the street, and wait.

CHAPTER

17

I folded the letter and stuffed it back in the bag. The streets were dark as I made my way to an intersection in a deserted part of town by the old park Bex and I used to frequent. I stopped and sighed. "What in the hell am I doing?"

"Coming to speak to Papa Legba." The voice spoke from behind me. I jumped, spun around, and stared into the face an old black man wearing a straw hat and leaning on a wooden cane. My attention was diverted to the black dog sitting beside him.

"Who are you?"

"I, dear boy, am Papa Legba." He laughed, blowing smoke into my face from a dark cherry wood pipe. He grinned at me. "Do you have something for me, son?"

I stared, shocked, and then regained my composure. "Uh, sure...." I dug around in the bag, pulled out his offerings, and placed them on the ground. The dog sniffed them, then sat back down. The old man looked at them, then at me. "Fine offerings; now what would you like to ask of me?"

I placed the backpack over my shoulder and stuffed my hands in my pockets. "Sir, I would like to speak to Ogun."

"Why?"

Stunned at his question, I stuttered, "I don't...really...know. I was informed it would help me heal."

The black smoke swirled around me and wrapped around my neck as he stared off down the street. "Why do you need to be healed? Why have you come to me in a state of uncertainty"

"I really don't know. I just thought I would try. Besides, I had a voice call out to me."

He nodded. "Is that so?" He puffed and blew smoke that this time turned into an army of creatures, but no warriors. I waited for him to speak again. After what felt like an eternity, he spoke. "Well, it seems as if Ogun does wish to speak to you and help you. So I grant my permission to seek him out."

"Thank you," I said as he disappeared, along with his offering, before my eyes.

"What the hell?" I rubbed my eyes in disbelief, but headed off to the park Bex and I had frequented.

As my feet crunched along the grass I thought of all the possibilities I had to end it all. Once I was deep amidst all the trees, I looked around. I opened the bag from Milly and saw a few containers with food. On top of the items sat another folded piece of paper.

If you have received the blessing from Papa Legba your journey is to continue. Jax, I know this is not the usual thing, but I promise Ogun can show you what a true warrior is. Offer him the food and the rum and ask him for guidance.

Opening them up, I saw roasted fish and plantains, as well as a cigar. Then I pulled a bottle of rum from the bag. I placed all the items on the ground and leaned them up next to a tree stump. Because I hated the idea of killing animals, I relented and found a small snail beside a tree. Taking it in my hands, I said a small prayer and crushed it. "Why me? Why has God taken everything from me?"

"God has taken nothing from you," a loud voice echoed amongst the trees.

I turned around and saw no one. What the fuck? Was I going crazy?

"No, you aren't going crazy."

I blinked, and before me stood a huge man...no, a warrior. His bare chest heaved and the clothing around his waist was like nothing I'd ever seen before. He wielded a huge machete. I stepped back and fell over a root in the ground.

"Do not be afraid."

"Who are you?"

"I am Ogun, a warrior much like you. You are here to speak to me?"

"I...uh...am?"

He smiled. "I'm glad you heard me call for you tonight." He looked up through the trees at the moonlit sky. "Tonight is the night that the most decorated warriors walk the earth. My brothers, your brothers, all who have given their lives to protect those they love, and for freedom."

A cold sweat covered my body. "Wait...am I dead?"

He laughed, and the sound ricocheted off the trees. "No, you are not dead." He glanced down at all the items on the ground. "You brought me a fine array of offerings. This is all for me, right? There is not another loa you have come to call on." He eyed me.

I shook my head and braced myself on the huge oak tree to my left. "No, I...don't think so."

His laugh boomed through the trees, making the birds chirp and flutter off through the air. "Why are you here, warrior?"

"I'm not really sure."

He scooped up the fish and took a bite. "You must have some idea why you have called on me."

"Well, it's actually you who called me."

He glowered at me. "Do not speak to me like that."

I backed up from the angry loa. "I guess for guidance on how to continue my life as it is." I patted my leg.

"Ahhh, but you are still a warrior."

"No, not anymore."

"Jackson Ledet, you will forever be a warrior, and a hero to the people that you fought for. Your service has never been forgotten." He puffed on the cigar.

"But I'm only half a man."

"No, you are a warrior," he corrected me.

In the distance, an apparition flew around the trees, back and forth. "What the hell?" Then a few dozen or so figures came into view, all dressed in different warrior garb. "What is this?" I asked.

The loa laughed. "Do not be afraid of those that have fought as you have, but lost more than a part of them."

"Was that a ghost? Are they ghosts?"

"If that's what you want to call them. I prefer brothers in arms; fellow warriors."

I didn't know what to think. Maybe I was still in my room and my mother had drugged the food I ate. I shook my head, trying to wake up from this dream.

"You aren't dreaming, Jackson. The only thing I can tell you is don't give up on life. But better yet, don't give up on love. It is important in this realm of yours. You have people that love you and want what's best for you. Remember what is on the other side may not always be the best decision. Your God would tell you the same thing as I do. Now hurry and go back home. But be kind to that companion of yours. A dog's love is like no other. He will help you heal."

"How did you know I had a dog?"

But he never answered me because he'd disappeared, taking all the offerings with him.

I shook my head. "This can't be happening." I walked back to my truck, and when I sat behind the wheel my head spun from recent events. Slowly I pulled the truck away and headed home.

The house was quiet as I made my way inside. I opened the door to my room and on the bed lay Bullet, snoring loudly. I scooted him over, and as soon as I lay comfortably in bed he nuzzled beside me.

CHAPTER 18

I woke to a small paw in my gut pushing on my abdomen. I rolled over but a yip stopped me. "Oh damn, I'm sorry, Bullet." He rolled over on his back, his little legs waving in the air.

Suddenly I remembered my weird ass adventure from last night. Could it have been real? "Nah. No way. It had to be a dream." Bullet rolled over and kicked his three legs up in the air, so I scratched his belly. "How about you and I take a walk and maybe play fetch?"

"Woof woof."

I shoved the blanket off us and chuckled. "Oh all right, we'll go. First I need to get showered and dressed." He rolled back over and snuggled into the pillow. "You go ahead and get a little more rest." I crawled out of bed and headed to the shower.

Without my leg on I hopped over to the bathroom, holding onto a chair by the bathroom door. Once my shower was done I looked into the mirror and stared at my reflection, then turned and faced the door.

When I walked outside of the bathroom, Bullet met me at the door and cocked his head at me. I rubbed the towel on my head to finish drying my hair. "You ready to go?" He jumped around like a kangaroo with pent up excitement. "Okay, hold on, let me get dressed."

He sat there and wagged his tail, watching me intently. I balanced on one leg and sat in the chair beside the bathroom door. I pulled my prosthesis around and began hooking it to the stump that used to be my leg. The whole time the puppy stared at me. He even crawled into a laying position and reached out with his paw to tap the outside of my leg. But quickly he pulled back. "No, it's okay, you can touch it." I pushed the prosthesis toward his paw. He touched it quickly, then drew his paw back. I slipped a pair of jeans on then stood, pulling the T-shirt on the back of the chair over my head. "All right, let's get going. I'm sure you are hungry too."

We exited the room and the house was quiet. Bullet ran down the steps, tumbling down the last two. "Be careful, little buddy." He righted himself, sitting on his rump with the one leg stuck out in front of him. He looked up at me and licked one front paw, and then the other.

I walked down the steps and patted him on the head. "Yeah, I know, buddy; you meant to do that."

After we'd both had a bite to eat, I clipped the leash to his collar and headed outside, where I looked up into the cloudless sky. "Bullet, it looks like a perfect day for a walk to the park." He looked over his shoulder at me, then proceeded to pull with such force, something I hadn't expected from this little guy on only three legs. "Hold on, little fella." He stopped, looked at me, then sat on his haunches.

We headed towards the truck and he sat waiting for me to open the door. As soon as I did, he placed his big paws up on the floorboard and tried to wiggle his back end up into the vehicle. "Wait, I'll help you." I pushed his butt up into the truck. Bullet scrambled up on the floorboard then lifted himself onto the seat. Once he was sprawled out on the passenger side of the bench seat, I scooted inside. After shutting the door, I started the ignition and pulled out onto the gravel driveway towards the park.

I looked at the puppy who had his paws on the passenger door, looking out the window. "You ready, little buddy?" He turned and looked at me and barked. I drove through the neighborhood and headed into town. Bullet braced himself on the door and balanced on one leg, his tail going about as fast as it could. His nose marked up the windows with nose shaped smudges. Goodness, I hoped that door was closed well; I would hate if he fell out.

Arriving at our destination, I pulled the truck into a parking spot. The green grass called out to Bullet, because he began to jump about wildly at the window, barking at the birds in the distance. "Hold on, little man." Bullet bounded back and forth in the seat in anticipation.

As soon as I opened the door the dog crawled into my lap, begging to get out. I held him and stepped out of the truck. Gently I placed him on the ground. He shook his body, stepped into the grass, and tugged on the leash. "You want off the leash?"

He turned around. "Woof woof."

"All right, but don't run too far."

He took off, hobbling into the grass and stopping to sniff, then running again. I leaned back into the vehicle and as I watched him, someone caught my eye. Bex!

"No, this can't be happening to me. Maybe she won't see me," I mumbled, still keeping an eye on Bullet. But damn, he ran right to her. I couldn't move as she knelt down then looked over at me, a grimace spreading across her face. "Well shit."

I walked over to Bex and Bullet. Bullet jumped up and down, brushing his paws on Bex's pants, begging to be held. I brushed a hand over my head and sighed. "Hello, Bex."

"Hello, Jax." She turned away from me.

Bullet sat on his haunches and looked at the both of us. "Woof."

"Look Bullet, we need to get going and leave Bex alone."

She nodded. "Yes, I agree...you should leave." She leaned down and petted Bullet, and whispered to him. He tugged on her pants leg.

I patted my leg. "Come on, Bullet, let's go." He whimpered but left with me, continuing to look over his shoulder at Bex. As I sat down beside a tree, Bullet came over to me and tugged at the ball in my hand. "Not now."

He gripped the ball and growled.

I looked down at him, him balancing on three legs with half the ball in his mouth. "Hey, little man, you doing good with your injury? Because I'm not." He stopped tugging, sat down, and looked at me, and I laughed. "Okay, so you wanna play?"

He bounced around me, balancing on his two front legs.

"Okay, then let's do this." I stood and tossed the ball a few feet, and away Bullet ran, his little butt up in the air as his pace quickened.

"Bring it back, boy. Come on, bring it back." He scooped it up and ran straight back to me. But instead of dropping it, he held onto the ball. "Come on, I'll throw it again." He wagged his tail and then dropped it. "Good boy." I threw it again.

After at least a dozen times my arm ached. "Hey, Bullet, what do you say we take a short walk?" He pranced around me with the ball in his mouth. Then I noticed he looked off to the left.

Bex was sitting there watching us. He ran off towards her with the ball in his mouth. I ambled over to them. "I'm sorry, Bex, if he is bothering you."

"He's not bothering me." Her voice was different and soft, not filled with the anger she'd expressed since I'd returned home. Bullet sat between us, his head playing tennis as he watched us.

He whimpered then barked loudly. I chuckled. "Um, Bex, I know this is out of left field, but it looks as if Bullet wants you to go on a walk with us."

She smiled for a split second, then her face faltered. "Oh, I don't know. I'm still mad at you."

"I know, but do it for Bullet."

She raised a brow. "For the dog?"

I glanced down at the puppy who sat wagging his tail. "See, he wants you to go on a walk with us."

She smiled. "Oh he does, does he?"

"Yes. And you wouldn't want to disappoint him, now would you?"

She grinned. "Well, I guess no harm done if I go for Bullet."

We walked through the trees until we reached the train station. I stood on the wooden planks staring across at the old building. The neutral toned brick building had remained the same since the day it was built. Looking up at the wrought iron rafters, it was as if time had stopped in a much simpler time.

Bullet bounded straight to the tracks. "No boy!" I ran after him and scooped him up in my arms. "You could get hurt."

"Woof!" He snuggled into my arms.

A train chugged up and stopped, the wheels screeching to a stop. Sadness crept through me as I remembered the two times I'd ridden on this train. As I contemplated life I sat down, Bullet nestled beside me staring up at me, but my thoughts were elsewhere. Of a much easier time before all this, I glanced down at my legs dangling over the edge of the wooden platform. Bex's hand rested on my arm. It was evident how much this woman could feel my pain without any words spoken. "This Bullet, is the train that brought me home." He faced me and dragged his tongue across my face. "You want to get something to eat??"

"Woof."

I nudged Bex. "Want to go to Ada Mae's and get something sweet?"

"Why not? But only for Bullet. Besides, I've got a hankering for a chocolate cream puff." She grinned up at me.

"Fine." I grabbed her hand and she pulled away from my grasp. My heart lurched forward at what I'd done. "I'm sorry."

"It's okay, let's just go."

She started walking and Bullet jumped from my arms and followed Bex.

Even before I opened the door to Ada Mae's, the smells of fresh baked bread and sweetness drifted around us. I held the door for Bex but Bullet ran inside, skidding to a stop in front of the glass counter. He tried to stand and place his front paws on the glass, but he kept falling over. On his last attempt his tongue slid down the glass as he toppled over. "Hold on, little buddy." I laughed as I picked him up.

The owner stood there tapping her toe. When I looked up, she smiled.

"Well, well, if it isn't Jackson Ledet, as I live and breathe. I'd heard you were back in town."

I held Bullet in my arms. "Yeah, I'm back. Sorry about this little guy; he's unstoppable." I patted his head and he barked.

She petted Bullet, "Like you are as well, I see."

Bex walked up to us. "Hey, Mary."

"Hey Bex. Are y'all back—?"

She interrupted Mary. "Hey, can we get a couple of chocolate cream puffs and two coffees, please?"

"Sure thing." Mary turned on her heels and headed back behind the counter. I nervously played with the silverware, tapping it on the metal table.

"Jax, stop it!"

I dropped the spoon and burst out laughing, then she did as well. Bullet sat on the floor looking up at us. Bex dropped her head and a wave of sadness overwhelmed me. "I'm sorry—"

"Two cream puffs and two coffees." Mary interrupted us and smiled. Then she knelt down and handed Bullet a cookie in the shape of a dog bone. He sniffed it then bit into it, causing a dozen or so little pieces to fall on the floor.

I watched as Bex ate, but couldn't touch mine. My heart was in pain, a pain I'd caused for the both of us. But seriously, what else could I do? This beautiful woman deserved so much more than me.

I caught Bex staring at me. I smiled when I saw a bit of chocolate on her lip. Reaching over, I wiped it off with my finger and she pulled back.

"What are you doing Jax?"

"Nothing. Sorry," I stammered, knowing I had made my bed. Maybe she was finally moving on...which was good. But damn, this woman's smile, the curve of her lips, did things to my brain, causing me to not think straight.

"Jax, I think I should be going."

I stood as she got up from the table. "Do you want me to walk back with you?"

"No, I need to be alone. Thanks for the afternoon. It was like old times." She smiled, but it was tinged with sadness.

Bullet pranced around me, being careful not to trip me. We headed back to the truck. The thought plagued me that I needed this puppy more than even I completely understood. His happiness radiated around me. "Hey Bullet, what do you say I ask Doc if I can adopt you? Would you like that?"

"Woof woof."

I scratched him under his chin. "Then I'll ask tomorrow."

CHAPTER

19

The next morning Bullet and I stepped inside the clinic and were met with instant chaos and barking. We walked further inside. "Hello," I hollered. No one answered my calls. Bullet raced off towards the back on three stubby legs.

I looked around and sniffed, and panic ensued as I smelled smoke. All of a sudden I heard barking behind me and I turned around. Bullet came running towards me. "What's wrong, little man? Hello!" I bellowed again. Then the smell of smoke wafted around me. "Oh shit, Bullet." I ran, followed by my companion.

Further back inside the clinic I could hear the crackle and pop of the fire. Over by the door to the kennels lay Doc. In an instant, I ran over to him. "Doc, Doc, hey are you okay?" He stirred a bit but didn't open his eyes. I bent down and checked his pulse, which was strong. I palmed my cell and quickly dialed 911. When the operator answered, I frantically spit out into the phone. "Fire at the Hutchinson Vet Clinic. Hurry."

"Sir, I'm dispatching the EMT and fire department now. Please stay on the phone."

Exasperated, I said, "I don't have time. I need to save the animals, Doc, and Milly." I barely finished and hung up, shoving the phone into my pocket. As I stared down at Doc, he started to come around and coughed. "Are you okay?"

"Yeah, for now. But Jackson, we need to get the animals out."

"I know, but first you and Milly." I helped him up, and as I did he draped an arm around me. My leg wobbled and I stumbled a bit. *You can do this*, I told myself. I balanced myself and gripped him harder, took a step, then another. After a few steps, I had to rest.

"Jax, only a few more steps."

I nodded and walked the rest of the way, holding on to Doc. Finally, determination took hold and I exited the building. Once we were a good distance from the burning building, I helped him down on the ground. "I'll be right back," I said, and went back in search of Milly.

On the floor, a shiny metal object caught my eye. Oh shit, the bracelet I'd given Bex on our first anniversary. She was here somewhere. "No, she can't be...she was taking some time off," I told myself. I began to run back inside, hardly touching the ground.

As I flew inside my heart pounded, and deep down the pain erupted. I couldn't take it if something happened to Bex.

In the distance the sight of a body caught my eye...Milly. I scooped her up and headed outside again. As I placed her in the grass beside Doc, I looked around and the silence was deafening. "Doc, keep an eye on her. I need to get back in and get the animals out."

"I'll help." He started to stand but wobbled.

"No, you stay out here and watch for the fire department." He sat back on the grass next to Milly. She began to come to, her eyelids fluttering, and coughed.

My heart beat so hard I swore at any moment it would pound right out of my chest. I had trouble breathing and I choked. Where in the hell was the fire department? I could see flames escaping from the building in front of me. I raced back inside to get the animals to safety.

The moment I opened the door to the kennels, the silence was eerie. As I walked in a few dogs barked, but not the usual piercing barks that penetrated my eardrums. Without hesitation I began unhooking all the latches on the cages. I swung each door open and the dogs raced past me. I continued unlocking the kennels, hoping they were getting safely outside. But soon my question was answered. Bullet barked, leading the dogs outside.

As I finished unlocking the cages I noticed some of the dogs were laying on their sides. I picked two little ones up and ran outside, placing them beside Doc to check on. He had his stethoscope out doing a preliminary triage on each one. I ran back inside and grabbed a couple of cats, then back outside I went, placing them on the ground. "Okay, Doc, that's the last of them. By the way, is Bex in there?"

"She shouldn't be. I think she left after picking up a few of her things."

I shook my head. "But are you sure? I saw a bracelet on the floor that I'd given her."

"No Jax, I'm not sure. I didn't see her leave."

I decided to make one last trip in another attempt to search for Bex, just in case. In the distance sirens wailed, so I limped inside to find her. I had to...I couldn't lose her.

"Bex!" I screamed, my voice becoming hoarse. I coughed and the smoke began to burn my eyes. I braced myself with my hands on my knees. My leg wobbled a bit, exhaustion, along with the smoke, consuming me. "Bex are you...," *cough*, "...are you here?" Flames flared up along the wall and I staggered, then Bullet stood by the wall, barking.

"Woof Woof!" Bullet ran towards me and grabbed at my pants leg.

"Hold on, little buddy, we need to get Bex." He tugged on my pants leg, then let go and ran across the room, dodging small flames on the floor. He raced toward the back wall, but a part of the ceiling crashed down to the floor. I followed him and saw her, my Bex. "No! Bullet!" I screamed. He skittered around the fallen rafter and made it to Bex, and lay beside her. I crawled on the ground to get away from the thick smoke. My eyes and throat burned, but I had to get Bex and Bullet.

When I reached Bex I checked her pulse. Thank goodness she was still alive.

"Jax?" Her eyelids fluttered as she said my name.

"Yes Bex, Bullet and I are here to save you. Come on, Bullet." I started to drag Bex towards the door, making sure to be careful with her. I kept an eye on my dog as he crawled on his belly. The heat intensified, as did the flames. My body ached but I couldn't stop now; I had to get us out—all of us. But when I reached the door it was barricaded by debris. I scooped Bex up in my arms and carried her over the parts of the ceiling that blocked our way. I looked back and saw Bullet struggling to crawl. "Come on, little buddy, you can do it."

A slight whimper escaped him. He looked up at me and moved his front paws forward. I coughed a bit and my head got fuzzy. I couldn't stop...I had to get us out of there. "You wait here, Bullet...I'll come back for you." I trudged over the debris and pushed the door open.

As the cool air hit me a fireman came over to me. "Are you okay, sir?" He lifted Bex from my grasp and I tumbled to the ground. "Is anyone else in there?"

I nodded. "My...dog...please save him."

CHAPTER 20

Beeping sounds woke me and I shot up in bed. "Calm down, Jax."

That voice...oh God, that voice. I grabbed Bex without even thinking and claimed her lips, those soft lips. Tasting her again, my tongue delved into her mouth. Our passion ignited and I felt as if my world was right again. What the fuck was I thinking, letting this woman go?

"I'm sorry, Bex." I held onto her, sniffing her jasmine scented hair. "The thought of losing you...I'm so sorry," I repeated. I rubbed my hands down her back and pulled her closer. Her chest close to mine, I was sure she could feel my heart beating. Her breasts pushed into my body. I needed to feel her, to claim her once again, to show her how much I desperately needed her.

She pulled back from me, her face flushed. Then I sensed a fuzzy black and brown head in my lap. "Hey, little buddy. You're safe."

"Yes. I heard from the firemen as soon as you hit the ground that they saw him crawling from the clinic. Apparently, he sensed you were hurt so he needed to be there for you. He wouldn't let you out of his sight; even barked, insisting he ride in the ambulance with you."

"Woof," he barked, and I petted his soft head.

"Thank you for saving me. Now for you." I faced
Bex and she smiled. "How are you feeling?"

"I'm okay, just a little smoke inhalation." She coughed.

"Are you sure? What did the doctors say?"

She laughed. "They said I would be fine, as would Doc and Miss Milly. If it hadn't been for you I don't think we would have survived."

"Good, I'm glad you are okay. But Bex, can I ask you something?"

She nodded. "Of course. But first, do you realize you are a hero?" My head dropped, but she picked it up and gazed into my eyes.
"Jackson Ledet, you saved us, along with all the

animals in the clinic, and you did it with no thought and one leg."

I grabbed her hands in mine, rubbing her palm with my thumb. "Do you forgive me?"

She raised an eyebrow and smirked at me. "For what, Jax?"

I knew she wanted me to admit how wrong I'd been. I sighed. "Bex, for being the biggest jackass of all time."

"And...?" She prodded me.

"And for letting you go for what feels like forever." I grinned at her.

She tapped her finger to her lip and eyed me. She then turned her back. "I don't know, Jax. What if you get a wild hair up your ass to become a jackass again?"

I chuckled loudly and removed Bullet from my lap, carefully placing him behind me on the pillow. I turned Bex to face me. "I can't promise that I won't," I smiled. "But I can promise to love you forever and to never ever let you go again." Bullet placed his paws on my back and barked loudly. Bex and I chuckled and he padded around and sat between us. "So Bex, do you?"

She nodded. "You know I do. I was just waiting for you to realize you were wrong to push me away. Jax, I love you no matter what. Two legs, one leg, I don't care. I've only ever had eyes for you."

"Bex, I love you too, and I can't tell you enough how sorry I am for sending you that letter." I pulled her closer to me, breathing in the sweet scent of jasmine.

She leaned into my embrace. "Just don't do it again. Let me in; remember I love you. I have your back, Jackson Hamilton Ledet."

"Woof!"

"So does Bullet," she laughed. The dog wiggled into my lap. Bex sighed deeply and petted Bullet. "I know your battle is a daily fight, and I'm here to tell you I will always be your cheerleader."

"Thank you for not giving up on me entirely."

She gazed into my eyes. "I know you are still healing and will continue to do so, but you must remember I'm here for you."

EPILOGUE

1 year later

I sauntered inside to grab a few drinks. After everything, I was finally happy and living the life I deserved. Those moments of self-hate still reared their ugly heads at me, but I had my family and Bullet to help me.

I glanced down at the tattoo that spread from my bicep down my forearm, which I'd gotten after I was released from the hospital after the fire. I rubbed my hand down the intricate design. It reminded me of who I'd been and who I was now. Up at the top white jasmine flowers wrapped around my bicep. They reminded me of Bex. The flowers extended down my arm ending at a paw print representing my unexpected hero, with one rose mid bloom representative of what I almost lost with Bex. And finally a rose in full bloom signifying what my life was now. Full of happiness and love.

The screen door slammed, pulling me from my thoughts. "Hey Jackson, great job out there, but your steaks are burning," Ben chuckled.

"Look man, you were supposed to be keeping an eye on them."

"Eh, I tried to, but that damn dog of yours is demanding when he wants to play fetch."

"Then what are you doing in here?"

"I came to check on you."

A knock sounded on the front door. "Be right there." I handed the drinks to Ben. "I'll be right out."

He nodded and headed outside, but not before swiping a hunk of cheese off the counter. I strode to the door and opened it. "Package for you, sir."

"Thanks, Bob."

"You are welcome. I hear it is a special something for that dog of yours." He winked at me.

"How…did…you know…? Never mind," I laughed, "Small town."

The mailman laughed. "Have a nice day, Jackson.

I walked back through the house and out the back door, letting the screen slam against the frame. "Bex, look what came in the mail." I held up the small box.

She held our daughter on her lap and clapped her hands. "Great, it's about time it came," she exclaimed, her lips forming a smile that I saw my daughter had inherited.

"What is it?" Ben asked, coming to stand behind me with a plate of food in his hand.

"As if you don't know, Ben. Everyone here knows but Bullet."

At the sound of his name, he dropped his ball and raced towards me, stopping right at the toe of my boot.

"Woof," he barked, wagging his tail. Then he stood in what my lovely wife called his second position stance.

"I had to beg the commanding officer to make it and send it here." I ripped open the box and a small chain with two silver dog tags dangled in my hand. Etched into the metal was:

Private Bullet Ledet
US Army

Below, our address was listed in case he got lost. As I leaned down to Bullet, I saw the blue eyes of my daughter and kissed her cheek. "Hello, beautiful."

"Woof woof." Bullet sat on his haunches and wagged his tail.

"Oh, all right buddy." I removed his collar and hooked his dog tags onto it. Once I clipped it back around his neck, I petted his head. "This makes you official."

"Woof."

The people in the backyard erupted into laughter.

In the distance I spotted a figure standing amidst the trees...he stood as tall as one of them. His stance was one of a warrior, his outfit the same, but not of this world. Then it hit me; he was Ogun, the same man Miss Milly had sent me to speak with. I rubbed a hand over my head. No, it couldn't be...that was a dream.

"Do you really think so?" Miss Milly said from behind me. I turned to face her and she smiled. When I turned back to the trees Ogun waved at me, then slowly faded away.

Voodoo Vows

Voodoo Vows 1

Ghosts from the Past— A Voodoo Vows
Short Story

Magical Memories— A Mother's Day
exclusive Short Story

Black Magic Betrayal- Voodoo Vows 2

The Guardians – A Voodoo Vows Tail

Bred by Magic

Gifted by Magic

Crescent City Sentries

Stone Heart- Crescent City Sentries Book 1

Coming Soon

Spell Bound Sacrifice Book 3 in Voodoo
Vows
Trapped by Magic Book 3 in The Guardians
The Gryphons Revenge Book 1 in BOA MC
Stone Player Book 2 in Crescent City Sentries

About the Author

As a young girl, Diana Marie Dubois was an avid reader and was often found in the local public library. Now you find her working in her local library. Hailing from the culture filled state of Louisiana, just outside of New Orleans; her biggest inspiration has always been the infamous Anne Rice and her tales of Vampires. It was those very stories that inspired Diana to take hold of her dreams and begin writing. She now has many other stories formulating in her head.

Amazon Page: http://www.amazon.com/-/e/B00O97TWUO

Facebook: https://www.facebook.com/diana.m.dubois

Goodreads https://www.goodreads.com/author/show/7690662.Diana_Marie_DuBois

Instagram: http://instagram.com/dianamariedubois

Pinterest: http://www.pinterest.com/dianamdubois/

Twitter: https://twitter.com/DianaMDuBois

Website: www.dianamariedubois.com